GW00703515

30127 05803850 1

On Torquemada's Sofa

ALSO BY LAURENCE FLEMING

Fiction

A Diet of Crumbs
The Heir to Longbourne

Non-fiction

The English Garden (with Alan Gore)
The One Hour Garden
Old English Villages (with Ann Gore & Clay Perry)
Roberto Burle Marx: A Portrait

ON TORQUEMADA'S SOFA

Laurence Fleming

BLACK
SPRING
PRESS

Published in 2005 by Black Spring Press Ltd
Curtain House
134–146 Curtain Road
London
EC2A 3AR

www.blackspringpress.co.uk

ISBN 0-948238-33-X

A full CIP record for this book is available from the British Library

Cover design Angela Lee and Paula Larsson

Typeset in Sabon by Dexter Haven Associates Ltd, London
Printed and bound in Great Britain by TJ International, Padstow

to
Igor & Ginger

CONTENTS

I

BRIDGET

Got it.

I have got it.

The one comfortable chair in the room.

Fits my bottom like a belt. Strange to think I used to wear one. Madame Vivienne she was called. At the bottom of Bond Street. We must have been rather rich then. Nothing ready-made for us. But of course with those clothes one did have to have a small waist. Cinched in I think. Now the war's over, darling, you can have a proper figure. A girl in your position shouldn't wobble. Really Mother was a fool.

And why, I ask myself at my present great age, does one never realise how stupid one's parents are while one still has them? Nothing between Father's ears but a wild hollow moaning and Mother's most serious reading was Angela Brazil. Quite like Angela Brazil myself. Fifth Form at St Dominic's or something. And where do we find ourself now? In the fifth form at St Dominic's.

The Green Group. Once again the Green Group. Our eighth meeting. Group therapy they call it. Rather like the Oxford Group in a way. All telling each other our sins. Except that we don't. Gradually, gradually, they trickle out, like a very long television series. All the facts in the last episode. And green only because we meet in this room. Nothing to do with being green. Not naive. Or environmentally friendly. How those advertising adjectives roll off one's tongue.

Not off my tongue, of course. Still having problems with it.

Green because of the carpet, an abstract masterpiece of the late Sixties. It looks like a well-kept lawn. Randal always cherished the lawn. But this one has had a bitch on heat spending pennies on it, at very regular intervals of course. Must be the ugliest room in the house. Copsewood. An ordinary monster miles from anywhere with two turrets and no flagpoles. And if, as Father would have said, a copse is a copse then it cannot also be a wood.

I must concentrate.

I must participate.

I must integrate.

Let's see who's talking. O dear, Clarissa. Clarissa the arch-bitch. No one is good enough for her. What a marvellous life she must have had to be as arrogant, as thoughtless and as completely self-centred as she is.

She can't be more than twenty-five. My daughter you might say.

Grand-daughter almost.

O dear God.

Clarissa: I didn't say anything of the sort. It was you – you, Mona – who said I must think about going on to Step Two. I haven't even taken Step One. If you think I agreed to come to this hellhole you're wrong.

Mona: But you must have agreed or you wouldn't be here. You must have admitted, at least to yourself, that your life as it was was becoming too much for you. That you wanted to change yourself.

Clarissa: No, no, it was everyone else who wanted me to change. I was perfectly happy living alone on Cloud Nine.

Mona: But you couldn't have stayed on Cloud Nine for ever.

Clarissa: Why not?

Mona: Well, the expense.

Clarissa: Never thought about it.

Mona: Then the waste.

Clarissa: Of what?

Mona: Of you.

Clarissa: I'm much more wasted here. Copsewood is not exactly a centre of creativity. Making something out of nothing you said yesterday.

Well, there's certainly plenty of nothing, five little male nothings scattered through this charming lounge. And your Step Two involves believing in something. A Power above ourselves. When we all know there isn't one.

Patrick: Speak for yourself, Clarissa. The power we're trying to escape from is much greater than ourselves.

Clarissa: So why try and escape from it? Being in someone else's power solves a lot of problems.

Patrick: They solve them, you mean. And it depends on the someone.

Clarissa: I really think I'm too old to believe in God.

Mona: No one is talking about God. Merely a power beyond ourselves.

Patrick: You can take your pick, Clarissa. Wodin, Thor, Dieu, Deus, Zeus, Allah, Jehovah, Apollo. Brahma. Vishnu. Shiva. Father Christmas.

Clarissa: Shiva, perhaps. The one who left his dick behind in an orchard? Worshipped all over India?

Patrick: Yes. Cut off by a furious husband.

Clarissa: So he hasn't got one?

Patrick: He grew another when he got back to – wherever he was staying at the time. And Shiva is the Destroyer. A really great power. Like the one we are trying to escape from.

Clarissa: So think of someone else as you seem to know so much.

Patrick: For you, Clarissa, Priapus. A disgusting old gentleman, seriously overweight, who walked around naked with an erection up to his chin. Son of Aphrodite and Dionysius.

Clarissa: Love. And Drink. I think I really could believe in that.

Layne: All old gentlemen is disgusting.

Not quite a conversation for me, I think. Even if I could think of something to say. Strange the way sex seems to permeate everything. Except my marriage, of course.

No kids, old girl. Either you get sewn up or I have 'em cut off.

I cannot get used to the idea that Randal is dead.

I think he could have said that before we married. Though I suppose I would still have married him. Honourable. Lieutenant-Colonel. So suitable. A green green girl. Wrong hole I said to him the first time. Not for me he said. So there it was. Nearly forty years. He. Is. Dead. One whisky too many. He was at my pills too. My lovely, lovely lily-of-the-vallium. How does this idiotic doctor think I can do without them? Thirty years. I have the most terrible dreams. It will be Priapus tonight I suppose. Why does Mona always pick on that wretched little Layne? She's supposed to be one of us. The disease. Not the doctor. Except that she's supposed to be cured.

I must speak.

Bridget: Layne. Name. Her call.
Mona: Did you say something, Bridget?
Bridget: Yes. Did. Layne is name her. Don't you call?
Mona: You're moving your lips but I can't make out the words.

Big effort now.

Bridget: Call her name. If that is her Layne.
Mona: That's much better. But you're still not making sense.

Not going to try again.

Mona: What you actually said was: Call her name. If that is her Layne. And her name is Elaine.

O dear. O dear O dear. Not going to say anything more. Why should it always come out backwards? My mind is clear. I know what I want to say. I want to say Mona you are a pop-eyed patronising little floosie no better than she ought to be and who comes from Stockport. Well, I know you can't help coming from Stockport, but you don't have to tell everyone. Those of us who do know where Stockport is would prefer not to. And those who don't know don't care. That awful little Darren doesn't know where Stockport is. Referred, I suppose. Juvenile

Court or something. Not so little either. Wouldn't at all care to be alone with him on a dark night.

I must stop. I must think beautiful thoughts. I am crying. I can feel them trickling down but I can't move. If I get up the chair will come too.

Take forty eggs and four pints of double cream, a gill of sherry. Separate the eggs and beat the whites until stiff. Beat the yolks until pale and combine with two pints of cream, then gradually stir the sherry into the mixture. Beat the other pints of cream until stiff but not buttery. Then very gently stir everything together with a wooden spoon and eat it entirely alone in the moonlight. I forgot the sugar. Two pounds of icing sugar would be nice. Beaten into the whites I suppose. Perhaps better into the yolks.

Randal didn't like the moon. When one comes to think about it, Randal didn't like anything. Randal was born in Kenya. Randal was a beautiful baby. So beautiful that some dreadful old witch doctor asked for a lock of his hair. But they gave him a piece of carpet fringe instead. The same colour of course. And the very same evening after dinner the carpet started to move across the floor. All by itself. And there was the old man in the bushes. Perhaps Layne is right. All old gentlemen is disgusting.

I feel so sorry for her. She really could be my granddaughter. A little lost soul terrified of everyone. I would love to put my arm around her and say There there it will all be all right in the end. But if I did she would just whip a stiletto out of her bra and plunge it into my bosom.

She couldn't miss that. They don't have bras these days of course. Where does she keep her stiletto? O dear. Not up there. It would be too painful. Must pay attention. Hammer and tongs again. Patrick and Clarissa. No bras because no bosoms. Girls don't have them any more.

Back to Madame Vivienne again. It will give Madam that gentle support just where she requires it.

Old witch. What she meant was that I was a flat-chested little virgin too shy to say No. Just like Layne. To say No to Madame Vivienne I mean. Never had the chance to say No to anyone else. Or Yes. And then we would go to Netta for the Fuller Figure for Mother. Also in Bond Street I think. Wish they were still there. Fifty-two. Fifty. Fifty-four. How surprised they would both be.

Now concentrate, Bridget.

Clarissa: So what you are actually saying in your pompous prissy way is that there isn't a substitute for real life.

Patrick: Quite right, Clarissa. I'd no idea you were so quick.

Clarissa: The trouble with you, you and your lightning mind, is that you think there is such a thing as real life.

Mona: Well, Clarissa, there is. And what everyone here is trying to do is find their real selves so that they can lead real lives.

Clarissa: And you're having a real life, are you, Mona? Our wise and experienced counsellor? You're just getting your rushes another way – being a sort of psychological Lady Bountiful. Haven't you got another skirt? That isn't even a real tartan.

Mona: No, I haven't got another skirt. Some of us had to pay for our own smack.

Gerald: M-M-Mona does n-n-neeed a new skirt. That one's very s-s-sexy. Goes well with her z-z-zip up boots.

Mona: Enough sarcasm for one day, thank you, Gerald. Though it's nice to hear you talking coherently. And just because you won't accept help it doesn't mean you don't need it. Shape up, as they say. Or ship out.

Clarissa: He can't do that. He's an assisted bed.

Mona: Sneaking, Clarissa. That was in confidence.

Clarissa: No secrets here, Mona. Bosoms bared. But it's good to think that Gerald's done something positive enough to get himself walled up here.

Gerald: Wh-wh-what's an assisted b-bed?

Clarissa: In House. That's what we are. In House. Now I have seen houses in comparison with which this is a simple beach hut.

Patrick: The Red Queen, Clarissa. So you have actually read something? And if Mona wanted a new skirt she would have to ask us all for permission.

Gerald: Wh-what's an assisssted bed?
Clarissa: Then let's talk about Mona's new skirt. Much more productive than discussing our motives and the person we ought to be.
Patrick: That's not why Daddy sent you here, Clarissa.
Clarissa: Never called him Daddy. You've got your generations mixed again, Patrick. Like everything else.
Layne: All Daddies is disgusting.
Clarissa: Layne has learnt a new word. With three syllables.
Mona: So at least something is happening.

I don't actually think, actually, that I need to listen to this far from fascinating conversation. Though there's no secret that Mona does need a new skirt. If I gave her one of mine she could make two. But that would be condescending of course. One must always remember how equal one is. Clarissa is amazingly beautiful considering everything. Not that one knows everything. But with that face, that figure and, presumably, that fortune as Georgette Heyer would have said, why did she have to take to speed or smack or smoke or whatever they call it? I wonder what she did call her father? Some sort of international polo player the grapevine says. With a stud in Suffolk. Lots of possibilities there.

Funny that this should remind me of those days in Ledbury. Long forgotten days. The Oxford Group they called it then. Father was caught first. First of all it was Mosley. Then it was Catholicism. Then Buchmanism. Then – nothing. Poor Father. But what could I have done? I think he really hated all women. But those house parties were amazing – the cook, the housemaids, the gardeners, all dragged into the drawing room to confess. Of course they didn't have anything to confess but he did raise their wages. Absolute what was it? Honesty, I think. Well that's what's happening here. No concessions to good manners here. No calling a spade a spade. Always a bloody shovel.

Then Purity, I think. So – absolutely no co-habiting of any kind. I wonder why the men are always going to the library. Unselfishness next, I seem to remember. So here we are more or less owning everything in common. No going out alone. No going about alone. Though they do of course. What would happen if we had to take a vote on Mona's skirt? And what would one recommend? She would look awful even dressed by Chanel. Awful in real clothes and awful in unreal ones. Like the ones she's got on. Oxfam I suppose. But there are Oxfams and Oxfams. You need to go to one in a good district. In the buff? Worse still I should imagine. I hope to be spared that. And the fourth thing was Absolute Love.

Patrick: No one is getting at you. No one is getting off with you. No one is trying to put you down. No one is against you. No one is ganging up on you. And no one is obsessed with you either. You are a cold-eyed, cold-hearted, calculating little vixen.

Clarissa: And with your brains, dear Patrick, I am sure you could put that into Latin and win a university prize.

Patrick: I've never been ashamed of being properly educated. Just as you've never been ashamed of your almost total ignorance.

Clarissa: And just exactly what use has your proper education been to you? You don't have to learn Latin or Greek or Geometry in order to learn how to paint. Even I can paint.

Dudley: Your fingernails at least. If nothing else.

Clarissa: So we're awake after all are we, Uncle Granpa? Thank you for your valuable contribution to our discussion.

Dudley: Your dispute.

Gerald: N-n-not a disp-p-pute. Bloody aaaargument. About as r-r-relevant to the m-m-matter in hand as –

Mona: What Clarissa is saying really is that no one has ever tried to find her real talents. And help her develop them. That's why she's here.

Gerald: C-c-can't remember. W-w-word's gone.

Patrick: Because she lives inside a barbed wire entanglement. Specially erected, and carefully maintained, to make any near approach impossible.

Dudley: Barbed wire keeps people in as well as out.
Patrick: As a great many men of your age must know.
Dudley: Yes. A great many. We have clubs and associations.
Clarissa: Called Alcoholics Anonymous.
Patrick: Clarissa, for goodness sake. You're here because you're trying to kick the most expensive habit of all. Smack and cocaine you said. Four hundred quid a day.
Clarissa: So?
Patrick: So don't look down your cunningly sculptured little nose at someone who found whisky cheaper. And just as effective.
Dudley: A triumph of the surgeon's art.
Mona: At least Dudley had a real life before he became dependent. You seem to have gone on to Cloud Nine straight from school.
Clarissa: Not school, Mona. College.
Patrick: Don't tell me you went on to higher education.
Clarissa: Certainly I did. Collège pour Demoiselles. Lausanne, Switzerland.
Gerald: And you started sh-sh-shooting up there?
Clarissa: Well yes. You see. There was this kinky old priest. Not so old actually. Your age, Gerald. But fatter. He just had this great passion for demoiselles.

Gerald: D-d-didn't think I could be sh-shocked any more.
Clarissa: Lucky still to be learning things at your age. We're still waiting, Layne.
Layne: OK. Kinky old priests is disgusting.

What an amateur these children make me feel. I was thirty before I began on my lovely lily. And on doctor's orders too. Under the doctor they call it. I cannot believe, I really cannot believe, that it was a priest who started Clarissa off. Shooting up is heroin I think. Injecting it straight into a vein. Rushing they call it. Or having a rush. I suppose I shall learn it all before too long. But do I really think that I am going to admit to all these people why I decided to come here? There's a marvellous new word. Can't quite think. Something in the Bible. Much prefer buggered. More direct. I am not going to get up and say. Well, I can't get up anyway. That for thirty years I was. That's it. Sodomised. I couldn't possibly say that word. All those little boys from Kenya probably grew up a bit odd. Not that there were many. Cocaine with their mother's milk, I suppose. Not that they got much of that I should think. And then sent home at five. Perhaps I was lucky he didn't want to tie me up first.

But O dear he was handsome. Mouth watering. I don't know why I never realised that those beautiful blue eyes had no expression in them. No warmth. Just fury occasionally. He would have hated his children. Nice to see that Layne actually smiled as she made her last remark. At least I think it was a smile. Not sure that I really want to know what she's been through. Though I suppose I shall have to. That's what it's all about.

I wouldn't mind being Clarissa. Or that's what I thought yesterday. Something has happened. I can't remember Step Two. Step One is just admitting that one is An Addict. Dependent Mona calls it. That we don't exist apart from whatever it is. Lily-of-the-vallium. So pretty. Wild at the bottom of the garden. Well, I've admitted that. Without it I feel like an Old Beached Whale. Or do I mean an Old Bleached Whale? Seem to remember Edith Evans. I look like an Old Peeled Wall. I don't do that. One's skin is still one's principal glory. And such a lot of it.

So I am doing all this to feel clean again. I feel dirty. Smirched. You have to be over fifty to have heard of that word. They never use it on telly. Always soiled or spotted. Of course if you're only soiled or spotted all you have to do is to get one of these magic new soap powders and give yourself a whirl in the washing machine. But smirching is more serious. It enters the soul. There isn't an all-purpose powder for souls. Yet.

Next step. Step Two, perhaps? I was a coward to have stayed silent for so long. What would Germaine Greer have said? Thank God I shall never meet her. And as for burning my bra. They would come down to my knees. And Miss Pirbright, who says she is Madame Vivienne's grand-daughter, would not be at all pleased.

She probably fire-proofs them anyway. There are a lot of regulations in this country that we know absolutely nothing about.

Clarissa: And in any case Patrick shouldn't be here at all. A misdiagnosis. He's not an alcoholic. He's a manic-depressive and there's no cure for that.
Dudley: Yes there is. Though not this one. And what do you know about it?
Clarissa: Nothing. Except that Patrick's either on an up or a down and they last for days at a time. With us you could have several ups in the same day.
Mona: Is it an up or a down day, Patrick?
Patrick: About half way up.
Mona: That's a good sign. If you were really depressed you'd have said half way down.
Clarissa: And what brings them on, Patrick? Do you ever know when you're going on a down?
Patrick: No. That is to say. No. Usually at the end of a wonderful up, often quite good. And then one morning, or one afternoon, or late at night, the fight just goes out of one. And you look at the paintings and think My God did I do that? And each one is worse than the one before.
Clarissa: So you go to bed with a bottle of whisky.
Patrick: A case if I'm lucky.
Dudley: And what happens to the pictures?

A long silence. Suddenly this is interesting. Patrick is terribly good-looking. Lean, dark and romantic just as he should be. Like Gregory Peck in *The Moon and Sixpence*. No one is speaking. Waiting. To hear what he's going to say. How wrong one can be about people.

Patrick: I chopped the last lot up. With an axe. Then had a bonfire. What I didn't realise was that it was four o'clock in the morning. So it was the police and the fire brigade and an ambulance before it had burned away. And as I still had the axe in my hand the police thought I was threatening them. So here I am.

It wasn't Gregory Peck. It was George Sanders and the picture burst into glorious technicolor at the end. And the paintings, which we hadn't seen before, were quite frightful. Really only fit to be burnt. I wonder what Patrick's were like.

Clarissa: But Patrick, isn't that like murdering your own children?
Janice: Yer. I were goin to say that.
Layne: Me too.
Patrick: As I've never had a child to murder I really can't tell you.
Clarissa: Perhaps Janice and Layne have?
Janice: No, no. They just thought so.

Layne: I'd like to ave one though.
Clarissa: Poor little thing. What happened then, Patrick?
Patrick: Magistrates Court. Bound over. Remanded for a medical report.
Dudley: But it can't be against the law, even in this country, to destroy your own work. Or even to hold bonfires in the middle of the night.
Patrick: It was a smokeless zone. And I probably smelt a bit.
Clarissa: Only of whisky, surely.
Patrick: No, it was meths. And I'd used some to light the fire.
Dudley: You can't have got to meths yet, Patrick. You're too young.
Patrick: Well, I didn't like them much. There wasn't anything else.
Clarissa: I think I saw some of your pictures once. Didn't you share an exhibition with someone called Bartholomew Stirling?
Patrick: Yes. A disaster.
Clarissa: Yours were all red.
Patrick: Yes.
Clarissa: I was having a run round with Bartholomew at the time. His were all black. Black with a little tiny phallic symbol concealed somewhere in the gloom. Phallic symbol. A good expression.

Janice: So what's a phallic symbol then?
Clarissa: Anything that can be mistaken in the dark for the male sex organ.
Janice: Like cricket bat andles and plice truncheons?
Layne: Yer. An broom andles, towel rollers, carrots, parsnips. An leeks.
Clarissa: Leeks! I hope he cut the roots off first.
Patrick: Those red pictures were quite good. I have a feeling the ones I burnt were quite good too.
Mona: Tell us, Patrick. If you want to, that is.
Patrick: I don't want to.

Patrick is crying. That makes two of us. I can't stop. Ruining my blouse. Never really seen a man cry before. Randal always did at the Remembrance Day service. On telly, of course. He wouldn't go. Had to pretend I hadn't noticed. It was the waste, he said. Waste. Yes. Waste. All those wasted lives. Imagine if Janice and Layne do have babies. Single parents in some terrible tower-block bringing up the next lot of muggers, rapists and glue sniffers. At the public expense too. Sometimes one wonders if Enoch Powell wasn't right sometimes.

I must stop being so old-fashioned. I'm beginning to get that buzzing in my head. And that awful cold hand in my stomach. And then that sharp pain at my rear end. Cancer of the rectum, I suppose. Clarissa isn't quite so awful today. What's she hiding, I wonder. She acts as a sort of. That word has quite gone. Something to do with animals. The only one I'm really afraid of is Darren. He doesn't speak. Neither does Barry, not yet anyway. Big brawny Barry with brown biceps and a beaming smile.

I can't be losing my mind if I can say that. Think it rather. But Darren is so squashy. Dark and squashy. As if someone had stepped on him. I wish I could help Patrick. But if I can't speak to him, what can I do? Artists is queer cattle, Father used to say. Though he didn't mean queer in that way. Sad not to be able to use the word gay any more. Meaning gay I mean. Cattle. That was the word. Cattleist. Clarissa acts as a catalyst. Perhaps Father did mean it in that way. With him, one never knew.

Clarissa acts as a sort of catalyst. The kind of sentence one's elocution mistress might have made one say. I wonder if I was ever like her. Certainly never as slim. Marvellous legs. One thing about here is that there is some food. That Health Farm I went to. One glass of pure spring water and two Ryvita. You had to try and convince yourself that that was your lunch.

About that pudding. Is sherry really the right thing? Champagne would make the cream curdle. Think of curdling four pints of cream. I suppose it would make some kind of cheese. But sherry is a bit banal. And brandy. And all those liqueurs are much too sweet. Wine would curdle. Whisky out of the question. Rum, perhaps. Of course. Calvados. O how marvellous. Forty eggs, four pints of cream and a bottle of Calvados.

Gerald: But you're not g-g-getting P-p-patrick to talk. He's c-c-clammed up completely. So why should I spill the b-b-beans?

Mona: Not a question of spilling the beans. We only want to hear what you want to tell us. You don't seem to understand that we're all in the same boat. We're trying to help. Thank goodness you're much clearer today.

Gerald: You c-c-can't just s-s-say to a p-p-person 'Oy you. C-c-come over here and b-be helped.'

Mona: No, you can't. No one in this room thinks that. But if by talking things through we can help you to change your motives, to look at your life, yourself, in another way, then that's helping.

Gerald: And th-that sort of help I do n-not need. I never shot up. Only snorted. N-n-not an addiction.

Mona: So why are you wearing long sleeves? You can't come to a place like this covered in track marks and expect no one to notice.

Gerald: OK so sometimes. But it w-w-wasn't an addiction.

Mona: You could manage your life without it?

Gerald: Y-y-yes I could manage w-w-without it.

Mona: For how long? A day? An hour? An afternoon?

Clarissa: You're bullying him, Mona.

Mona: Some people only understand violence.

Clarissa: Only the thickest. Barry – and look at him grinning – and Darren. Gerald isn't that dim.
Mona: No one said Gerald was dim. But he's here to clear out a habit that's been running his life for several years. And the first thing he's got to do is to admit that.
Clarissa: Gerald has been posted in here by one of the million arms of Her Majesty's law to get him into a fit state to plead at his own trial.
Dudley: Has he, indeed? How very bizarre. What new way of spending public funds will they think of next, I wonder?
Mona: OK so yes he has. We don't want to know anything about that. We don't even want to know why he took to freebasing. Just to help him get over it. He's a sick person trying to get well. Not a bad person trying to be good.
Barry: Don't aveter say that every bloody day.
Mona: Shouldn't have to. But Gerald goes swanning around as if there was nothing wrong with him. Trying to make us all believe his being here is the result of a huge administrative error.
Janice: Right, Mona. Right, right. Gerald asnt never done nothing wrong in is ole life. Look at is empty face. Course e's juss a ministrative error.
Layne: I ad oner them too. Finished up in a ome.
Janice: An Darry. An Barren. They never did nothing wrong neither. All a big cock-up at the Security.

Barry: Weren't no big cocks up at my Security.
Clarissa: Just a great big phallic symbol yourself, Barry.

All these cult phrases. What can freebasing be? Snorting is just sniffing the powder up your nose. Sniffing is glue. Very non-U that seems to be. Shooting up is injecting it. So what is freebasing? Smoking perhaps. I am beginning to feel tired. Words will start coming in the wrong order soon. Perhaps I could have a little zizz. Don't think anyone would notice. So strange to be back at the beginning again. Absolute Love they called it. Of course Father couldn't manage that. If we had managed to stay within those four absolutes things different would have been. Of course I realise that now Randal didn't in anything believe. Not in him even. Self-knowledge. Awareness of self, the Buddhists say. All very close to each other the religions. Except Islam. Seems to be different a bit. Never read the Koran. Arabic so beautiful looks.

Concentrate, Bridget.

But I am off to sleep. Dropping. A haze falling. Beautiful mauve haze. Something about that colour. Soothing. Cool. Wild at the garden of the bottom. Lily-of-the-vallium. O my lovely lily. Why did they ever give me make it up? Never did no harm to no one. Janice is a caution. Copper hair. Legs. Never had legs. Better than Clarissa. Then at her face you look. Ravaged. Wrinkled. What can she through have been. Just slipping quietly away. Away slipping quietly just. Slipping just away quietly. Quietly.

Slipping. Just. Absolute love here by anyone doesn't know nothing about.

Barry: Weren't none er them. Acid, Gerald. Weren't it?
Gerald: Once.
Barry: I reckernise you. Party. Iston Waldy something. Grotty old manor. You an your friend was the only two in suits. Thought you was going to kill each other.
Gerald: T-t-try anything once.
Barry: What appened to im then?
Gerald: N-n-not sure.
Layne: Weren't only once, though, Gerald. It went on an on. You can tell always. Your eyes belongs to someone else.
Gerald: T-t-taking a good l-l-look at you though.
Janice: Well lucky little Layne. What's she done to deserve that, then?
Gerald: W-w-with a bath and her hair on s-straight Layne w-would be a knockout.
Mona: When Layne has a bath we'll know she's beginning to come back to life again.
Layne: An it's my air. An my teeth. All me is me.
Gerald: N-n-not the bit between the ears. They left that out.

Back to Father again. Why they can't drop me let off? My head. Pounding. Throbbing. And that terrible pain in the stomach. Four pints of cream. Cream of four pints. Pints of four cream. Of four cream pints. Like a mantra. Makes me feel better. Four pints of cream. Four pints of cream. Throbbing's beginning to go. Clearing. Clearing. Clearing. Absolute Honesty was the thing. Father took to it at once. Until someone Absolute Honestied him. A putrid old fart he called him. Cold and cruel. Father sacked him of course. Luckily the war started then so he went straight into the Navy. Carpenter, that's right. Estate carpenter. The most beautiful work. And very handsome. Brown biceps like Barry. He was called Douglas. After Haig. Of course there were no history books at the beginning of 1918. They couldn't have known. And then those words of Father's. Engraved.

The trouble with you, Matthew, is that you don't add up. You've no brains. You've been alive for seventeen years and you've learnt nothing. At colossal expense. You don't hunt. You can't shoot. Can't even fish. You have no skill, no information. You couldn't even do a job. You're a useless object eating four huge meals a day which I pay for. And what I really can't understand is that everyone seems to like you.

You can't fight that. That was when Douglas spoke up. We were all in his power. Mother as well. She could do nothing without asking him. I wonder if. Not a fool really. Much to be pitied. Change the subject. Father abandoned the Buchmanites. Bit too two-way for him. And after that he was against everyone. Particularly Mother. Particularly me, when I had to start cooking. No war service for me. Aged parents to look after. My lovely brother. Matthew. I wonder if Douglas and he. It seems very unimportant now. Never came back of course. We shall never know. I used to count the days until he came back from school. Until I was sent away myself. I think I really did love him. Only Missing. But he would have turned up by now.

Douglas was definitely lost. The Battle for Crete. So when Randal offered to take me away from all that I had to say Yes. At least it was a new kind of servitude. Jane Eyre. I think. But not a Mr Rochester.

What a shock for Matthew if he did come back. To find the house a bacteriological research institute. My God, if I can find those words, I must be mending. But I hate to think of all those little bacterias jumping about in my bedroom.

I wish I could stop crying. I don't want to say anything but I would like to be able to. They didn't look at all like Randal, either of them. Don't be so silly. Now the mantra again. Take forty eggs and four pints of cream. Take forty pints of cream and four eggs. Much better. It would take so long to separate forty eggs. Nothing else to do, though. And what I really can't understand is that everyone seems to like you.

I have grown into this chair.

It has put its loving arms around me.

I shall sit here and smile.

And pretend that everybody likes me.

Dudley: But you seem to be well-educated. Well-spoken. So what are you doing here at our expense?
Gerald: Clarissa told you. C-c-court case p-p-pending.
Dudley: And what sort of case is it?
Mona: We don't ask questions like that, Dudley. Too contentious.
Dudley: Well, I'm feeling a bit contentious. I don't mind paying for Janice and Layne, for instance. But Gerald should bloody well look after himself.
Janice: Not payin fer us, Granpa. We're private.
Layne: Gotter nangel you see.
Gerald: One in the. W-w-one in the eye f-for you. Old ch-chap. T-t-tell us ab-bout your angel. Wh-what colour are his?
Janice: Wings? Well, e's bald. An e's – well, plump to middlin. Got fat ands. Makes you shiver. Not old, really. It's not that e's past it exackly. More like e juss can't.

II

PATRICK

Layne: Into redeemin e calls it.
Dudley: The ultimate perversion.
Layne: O no e's not kinky. Least not what I calls kinky. Slong as e don't touch you it's OK. E's got pink glasses.
Gerald: H-h-how did he f-find you two b-b-beauties?
Janice: Not difficult. Spends is spare time trawlin the streets roun King's Cross. Like us. Smart word trawlin.
Clarissa: Meaning dredging, perhaps?
Layne: Calls us is little fishes.
Gerald: And when you l-leave here? Is he g-giving you a j-job?
Janice: Ope not. Works in some office. Town All or something.
Gerald: Then wh-what?

Layne: Goin ter send Jan ter college. Gave er a little test. Says she's got a IQ of undred n thirty.
Gerald: And wh-what's he doing for?
Janice: Layne? Goin to train er as a airdresser. Says she's got very gentle ands.
Gerald: H-how did he find th-that out, I w-w-wonder?
Janice: Or a masseuse.
Gerald: Isn't she th-that already?
Layne: Say it in me posh voice, shall I, Jan? That is not among the special services what I offer.
Dudley: One in the eye for you. Young man.
Clarissa: I think that's marvellous. Does he belong to some organisation?

Or is it just goodness of heart?

I shouldn't have told them about burning those paintings. At least, I should have told them rather more of the truth. Or should I? It was the house that burned down. The paintings just happened to be in it. I chopped them up. Just as I said I had. And started the fire with them but I don't think they can prove that. And I really thought the fire would have got me too. But some idiot of a fireman got me first. They made me thank him afterwards, smug bugger. You never saw anyone look so pleased with himself. I should have slashed my wrists first, I suppose. But it was a fire day, not a blood day. And you can bet your bottom dollar there would have been some highly qualified ambulanceman on hand to give me an absolutely enormous transfusion actually on the spot.

Why are they all so determined to save lives? They don't have to take the Hypocritic Oath.

Most people's lives are completely pointless. Unproductive. Unconstructive. I look at the crowds in London sometimes and think: what on earth are they all for? What is the point of the faceless millions? What do they achieve? What is their function? Nothing. Of course they haven't got one. The heavenly computer has just got out of hand.

I pressed the wrong button once and got two hundred and fifty copies of 'the quick brown fox jumped over the lazy dog'. It wouldn't stop. It couldn't stop. Just went on and on. Like the Sorcerer's Apprentice. Only the Sorcerer didn't come. Had to turn it off at the mains. But it's not dead. Just asleep or sulking. If I turn it on again it will spew out two million copies all in a moment. Like a salmon in milt. Or are computers hermaphrodite? I bet they are. So two million tiny little computers all crawling all over the floor and asking those absurd questions. It would take more than a sorcerer to sort that out.

But I wish he would come. Yes, sorcerers are hes. Shes are witches. Witches are shes. O God. As if I didn't know that. Stop thinking. You'll only start crying again. Stop. Stop. Listen to the scintillating converse flowing round you. I suppose we're all waiting for a sorcerer. Waiting for Godot. Perhaps that was what he meant. But we have to stop waiting. If the Sorcerer doesn't come, we have to turn sorcerer ourselves.

Well. A very good idea. What would I do to transform the people in this room, for instance? Actually, I would transform the room first. Those curtains. What could have been in the mind of the person who designed those curtains? Amoeba and phagocytes in bilious greens swimming through a sea of vomit. Very smart vomit, of course, the colour it goes after too much lobster and whisky. And what on earth is a phagocyte?

The old girl in the tub chair. But how can you force someone to lose six stone in weight? Impossible to know what she really looks like because she hasn't any bones. That show, that is to say. Must have been a beauty in her day nevertheless. Those eyes. Not totally piggied in fat. A really fantastic blue. Prussian and ultramarine three-quarters to a quarter, that would do it. But haunted. I don't want to paint haunted people any more.

I don't want to paint people any more.

I don't want to paint any more.

So what do I want to do?

Absolutely nothing.

Gerald: B-but it's n-not natural to w-want to h-help other p-people on that s-sort of scale. Of course he's perverted. That's how he gets his kicks.

Dudley: At least his kicks benefit someone, then. More than one can say for a lot of people.

Janice: So OK e's perverted.
Dudley: Perverted is a Latin word. It means turned aside.
Patrick: It means turned through. Inside out. Upside down.
Gerald: Turned aside's enough for me.
Janice: So what's all this Latin then?
Dudley: Language of the Ancient Romans, Janice.
Janice: Oo? Nero an that lot?
Layne: Yer. An is chum Callygooler. Ad a thing about orses.
Dudley: Who told you about Nero and Caligula?
Layne: Well we ad this client, didn we Jan? E called im Callygooler though. Way you say it makes it sound like some kinder posh flower.
Gerald: And w-what did this c-client want you to do?
Layne: Ad to tickle is throat wiv a fevver.
Gerald: Till he threw up?
Janice: Till e come off. Only took a minute most times.
Dudley: But did you tickle the inside of his throat?
Janice: What you want then? Blow by blow description?
Gerald: Yes, please. Blow by b-b-bloody blow.
Mona: If it would help you to tell us, Janice, then we're all willing to listen.
Janice: What you think, Layne?
Layne: Might as well. Can't urt im now.

Janice: Spose not. They got im. E were some kinder weird pusher. Didn supply us though. Least sometimes e did but e wernt our regular. Wanted to be a cock.

Layne: So you ad ter pretend you was a en broody on er nest. You ad to sing Cluck cluck I wants a fuck to the tune of God Save the Queen.

Janice: Then e'd come in wearing a black leather mask an a sorter red plastic frill on top. Like e were a cock like I said. I mean the bird fcourse. Not the phallic symbol. An e'd say Cock a doodle doo I'm goin to roger you.

Gerald: To what tune this time?

Layne: No tune. E just sorter said it. Starkers cept for a big red plastic dill down tween is legs an a bunch of fevvers up is arse.

Clarissa: Badly frightened by a feather duster at the age of three, I suppose.

Mona: No frivolous interruptions, please.

Gerald: G-go on.

Janice: E ad boots too, Layne, remember? Ridin boots with big spurs. Made im feel dominant I expeck. An e'd scatter sweets in fronter you which you ad to pick off the floor with your teeth.

Mona: What kind of sweets were they?

Janice: Fettamines ercourse. But we never swallowed em.

Layne: You could drop em down atween your tits and then ide em when e wernt looking.
Janice: Made a little pocket money for us.
Gerald: Go on, go on.
Janice: So oo's perverted now? If you think you can try anything like that ere better ave another think.
Layne: So then e'd crouch down on the floor an we'd tickle is back with our feathers.
Janice: Stuck up our arses.
Layne: Then e'd turn over an we'd tickle the fronter is throat. Squattin sorter. Over im.
Janice: An e'd pertend ter come off.
Gerald: Why only p-p-pretend?
Clarissa: Paralysed with hysterical laughter I should think.
Janice: Cos e couldn. E'd come in all tanked up an one day e juss passed out. So we ad a little look an there weren't nothin there.
Layne: Been cut off. Like that god.
Janice: When they caught im – whoever they were – they tarred an feathered im an set im alight.
Layne: So e jumped in the river an drowned. Nobody couldn reckernise im. But we knew.
Mona: How? Did you go to the police?
Janice: Said in the papers e was missin a vital organ. Can't be two men like that in one city. An we didn tell no one because we didn know oo e was

> in the firs place. Not is name. Never saw im
> again neither. Of course.

How old this makes me feel. Extremely old. Those girls can't be more than twenty, if that. Ridiculous to spend time thinking about artistic integrity with all this going on. Or worrying about whether I'm ever going to work again. Or get the fire insurance. They must have put their lives at risk every day of those lives. What an absurd thought for someone sitting here with a very sharp kitchen knife in his pocket. Just slipped in with some dirty dishes. Being helpful. And there it was on the table. Now it's snug in my pocket. I think. My God, it isn't. Other pocket? God, it's not. Now who, in this pathetic, down-at-heel, down-trodden congregation would be clever enough to pick my pocket?

When you look at them, they're sad. We're sad. Must be one of the boys as I haven't been anywhere near the girls since lunch. Not Dudley. A. he wouldn't want it and B. I haven't been within speaking distance all day. Gerald, well Gerald is very peculiar but I don't think he's light-fingered enough. You have to be quite experienced to pick a pocket successfully. Barry. Not Barry. He would just have knocked me out first. So it has to be Darren. Now what on earth would Darren want with a knife? He says nothing. You can't learn anything from looking at him. Dark. Damaged-looking. I would have said Welsh-looking but that's racist of course. Shifty? Not really. When he looks at you he really looks at you. Grubby jeans. Grubby T-shirt. Picture of a bomb-crater and 'I survived the Black Hole' written on it. Wonder if he can read? Looks like a survivor. Boneless. Strange that he can look thin and pudgy at the same time.

Anyway, I can hardly accuse him of stealing something that I stole myself.

Now that I look at him carefully, he's looking really worried. Green. Since Janice and Layne started telling us about their client. Some kind of a weird pusher, they said. Don't tell me Darren's a pusher. I wouldn't have thought he had that much initiative. Devious of course, but being devious isn't enough in that trade. What do I know about it? There is one person I would rather like to tar and feather. But set alight? Some really sick person there. A manic depressive perhaps. Not funny, Patrick. With a taste for arson. Not at all funny, Patrick.

So let us lean back into this extremely uncomfortable sofa and think about Leonora.

Mona: Patrick will answer that question in his own good time. No need to bother him now.

Clarissa: He is, as usual, entirely wrapped up in his own fascinating thoughts. It must be nice to be able to float away on to Cloud Nine without any external assistance.

Gerald: Don't th-think he's on Cloud Nine. Still s-sulking if you ask me.

Clarissa: Well, we're not asking you. What's he got to sulk about?

Gerald: You m-made him tell us about his b-b-bonfire.

Mona: That's what we're here for. To listen. We'll listen to you if you've got anything to say.

Gerald: I haven't.

Janice: So oo's sulking now, then?

Gerald: Not saying anything isn't sulking. Just being k-kind. If you've got nothing to say, sh-shut up.

Layne: Or it'll be taken down in evidence against you.

Barry: Right on. You as the right ter remain silent.

Janice: Course no one's never said that to us serious. We ad this client oo liked to be a pliceman. But we adter rest im an say them words.

Layne: Covered with red air. You could've scrubbed pots with im.

Janice: But thank God e never thought of that.

Covered with red hair. Not that she was covered exactly. Just in the right places. And not really red either. Vandyke and vermilion fifty fifty. Extraordinary to think that Clarissa saw all those paintings. Leonora by Firelight. Leonora in the Morning. Leonora in the Bath. Leonora by Lamplight. Leonora on the Loo. Square titles. Not square paintings though. Perhaps they were quite good. And then of course Leonora Dead. That was why the police turned up. Hoped they were going to say the exhibition was obscene. But no. Just that Leonora had been found in exactly that position with her throat cut. Grisly coincidence. Because all I did was to add a bit of red paint to Leonora in the Afternoon. She lay on the sofa in a particular way. And would I please go along with them to the station.

Dudley: Don't you think so, Patrick?
Patrick: Don't I think so what?
Mona: Ah.
Clarissa: Cloud Nine again.
Dudley: Don't you think this lust for equality is rather degrading?
Patrick: I suppose everyone being equal doesn't mean everyone has to be the same. Because this I will tell you. If you take an equal amount of every colour in your palette and mix them all together, you get a nasty greenish greyish brownish sludge.
Clarissa: A masterly description of our society in fact.
Gerald: S-sp-peak f-for yourself, Clarissa.
Clarissa: I am. Here we all are. The Sludge of Society.
Barry: No rude words ere if you please.
Clarissa: You don't even know what it means.
Barry: Dead right I don't. So don't call me that, OK? Might take offence.
Mona: It just means an amorphous mass of indeterminate colour. Nothing to take offence at.

Barry: Don't mind morphous. Or intermediate. But sludge is rude.
Mona: Clarissa was speaking metaphorically.
Clarissa: Quite right, Mona. Metaphorically.
Dudley: Does sludge mean something special that we don't know about. In your world, I mean, Barry?
Janice: No, it don't. Drudge, grudge, fudge. Sludge is a sorter cross atween a slag an a drudge.
Layne: Us all right.
Mona: But a person can't be a sludge. Sludge is a thing, a sort of stuff.
Barry: You a school teacher, Mona?
Mona: Yes. At one time. Primary school.
Clarissa: What useful experience for you.
Dudley: Equality is a mathematical concept. Nothing to do with people.Two does equal two, but no two people equal any two other people.
Janice: Why not? I bet Layne an I could beat Clarissa an Gerald at chess.
Gerald: W-winners and equals aren't l-losers.
Layne: An we can't really play chess, Jan.
Janice: We knows the rules anyow. We ad this client. An guess what e wanted er be? The Red Queen.

The Red Queen. O God, there she is again. O God. My God. Why hast thou forsaken me? There is something spooky about these people. Though Janice couldn't have known that I tried to paint Leonora as the Red Queen.

The amazing thing was that she was beautiful in any position. No matter how she arranged herself, or where, there was the picture. Florence Nightingale. Joan of Arc. The Red Queen, but not Alice's Red Queen. She wanted to be somewhere between Clytemnestra and Turandot though one can't imagine that either of them ever took all their clothes off. Then she wanted to hire the jewellery but I said No, I'm not a photographer. Of course I can make strands of tinsel look like pearls. So in the end she had pearls round her neck and all the way down her arms and nothing else. And she stood on red with red behind her. Hair piled up. Acknowledging the cheering crowds. Red, said Leonora, is the colour of love. But she was wrong. Love is black.

So I painted her black. Not her but her surroundings. Black with purple lights. It looked much better. But of course she didn't think so. She just took a kitchen knife and ripped it across and across and across and she held me off by throwing bottles at me, turpentine, white spirits, anything that came to hand and screaming at the top of her voice He's going to kill me help help help.

I would have done, too. If Marco and Nesta hadn't come up. Marco and Nesta. A very suspect couple. Said they were sculptors.

I remember saying: She's just murdered one of my children. Our children, she said. I wanted a red one and you gave me a black one. Mothers don't kill their own children, I said. Yes they do if they can't stand the sight of them. Give me the knife said Marco and we'll help you to clear up the mess. He can't do it Nesta she said. Look at him. Answer to a maiden's prayer you might think. But no. Get into bed with him and he goes rigid and starts sweating. All except the bit that you want to go rigid. She said it. She said it. She said it. That's why he calls these paintings his children. The poor sod won't ever have any others.

O God, I'm sweating now. Hands clasped together. Knees tightly crossed. Four years ago. Can it really be as long as that? Calm down, Patrick. Calm down. Calm down. Calm Down. Breathe. In for four. Hold for sixteen. Out for eight. One, two, three, four.

One, two, three, four, five, six, seven, eight, nine, ten, eleven, twelve, thirteen, fourteen, fifteen, sixteen.

One, two, three, four, five, six, seven, eight.

Now do it again.

And again.

Better.

Much better.

Four years. I can't believe it. They sold, all those pictures. The bubble hadn't burst then. People would buy anything. The North Sea Bubble you might call it except that it had nothing to do with gas. Property. She tried to deface them in the gallery but we were waiting for her. And then the police. She was found in exactly the position of one of those pictures with her carotid artery severed. A small neat surgical job. She must have paid someone.

I wouldn't have done that. I would have slashed her into a million strips. Just as she did to that painting. I had an alibi. An alibi provided by my brilliant brainy blameless boring banal barrister brother. Smug. Serene. Sensible. Successful. Simon.

O God don't let's think about him.

Let's try and think about them.

Mona: Because although Janice's memoirs are very interesting, they don't tell us anything about her.

Gerald: D-d-do. Tell us she's one helluva. Hell of an acc-accomplished little s-slut.

Clarissa: Don't agree. Janice had a very expensive habit. She needed at least two hundred quid a day. She could have stolen. That is, she could have tried. Instead of which she went to work, like a dishonest woman.

Janice: Well thanks tons Clarissa. Never expected a boost from you.

Clarissa: I admire that. I couldn't have done it. The money was there for me. All I had to do was spend it. Don't think I could have found a job which paid two hundred quid a day.

Gerald: Could have j-j-joined J-j-janice. I'd p-pay.

Clarissa: Well thanks tons Gerald.

Dudley: And where would you have got that sort of money?

Gerald: B-borrowed it, of course. As they s-s-say.

Barry: Yer, borrowed it. Got very good at borrowing. Bloody amazing the loot the gentry carries round on em. Acid parties was the best. Raised five grand once. Got away with it too.

Clarissa: That can't have lasted very long.

Barry: Didn need it every day. Ad a job as a bouncer. Punch-up as good as a snort. Cheaper, too.

Mona: Did you go into your punch-ups when you were high? Or were you high when you came out of them?

Barry: Depends. Sometimes I were an sometimes I wernt.

Dudley: Very graphic.

Janice: What the gentleman means, Uncle Granpa, is that on the days when e couldn get a fix e ad a punch-up instead. Very relaxing I expeck e found it. But on some days e ad a fix an a punch-up. Fore e went on acid that is.

Barry: An oo says I were on acid?

Janice: Don't go to acid parties juss to lift loot.

Barry: Dead right you don't.

Gerald: B-but could you forget anything after?

Barry: Course not. Could you?

Mona: So when you were on a trip – on a long trip let us say – you couldn't remember what you had done afterwards? or where you had been?

Barry: Right. Copper's nark, Mona?

Mona: No, Barry, I'm not. But I have no experience of acid so don't quite know what it does. If you're trying to help someone out of a habit, you have to know what the habit did to them.

Barry: Screws you up. Total.

Gerald: R-r-remember nothing after.

Barry: Can't remember nothing at all. Genuine.

Dudley: Sometimes very convenient, I imagine.

Clarissa: Barry has been referred, Uncle Granpa. He isn't quite sure why and they aren't either.

Dudley: That doesn't make sense.

Janice: Nothin does. They thinks a crime as been kermitted. They thinks Barry probly done it. So they opes when e's dry again e'll remember if e done it or not. Meanwhile the fuzz is tryin to fine out if an actual crime as been kermitted cos if it asnt then they can stop fussin.

Dudley: Who's they exactly?

Janice: Drug Squad I'd guess. CID praps.

Barry: Tax man.

Gerald: M-m-must be j-j-oking.

Janice: We ad this client pertended ter be a tax man.

Layne: No, no, Jan. Let's forget im.

Janice: Well e were very ugly. Barmy o course. But armless.

Layne: E was disgusting.

Janice: We ad to fill in a form an fiddle the famly lowances. An then e'd say you ave claimed for four children an a motor car but you only as two children an a bicycle. Bicycles are not tax deductible. You will go to jail for thirty years without the option of a fine.

Clarissa: And then?

Janice: Then e'd burst into tears cos e was bein so cruel. But Barry don't mean that. There's a mob after im.

Not the only one being pursued if he is. Exit pursued by the Furies. Exit pursued by a bear. But I, of course, distinguished me, am being pursued only by myself. Pursued by my own artistic integrity. Did my own thing. If an artist has a value, it is because he is not the same as everybody else. He has not allowed himself to become de-personalised. Or herself. How many millions of times have I said that? Only I don't believe it any more. I don't believe in anything any more. Death. What is the point of creating a thing, or a person, if they are going to be destroyed, or die, anyway?

A long way from birth to death. Just as far as from black to white. The entire spectrum. People talk in terms of black and white all the time today. As if there were nothing between fascism and anarchy. Between repression and obsession. Between a photograph and the totally abstract. But, as sanctified Simon so succinctly says, integrity has no value at the checkout point. Or job satisfaction. They need money. Everything is all about money.

Being very lucid all of a sudden.

If you throw all your furniture out of the window into your own garden nobody minds. But if you throw it on to the pavement you are breaking the law. Just imagine all those grey men in Parliament, brilliant Simon's benevolent friends, solemnly enacting a law which says: it is illegal to throw furniture on to the pavement. It constitutes an obstruction to a public right of way. So all right. After the first few tables I threw it all into the garden. Simon was kind enough to tell me about the law very soon after I started.

I am bigger than Simon. Older. Fiercer. Drunker. But darling you are such a disappointment to us. Simon is two years younger than you but he's in a higher form. Right at the top of it, too.

So we had to find something that he couldn't do. And he certainly can't paint.

And neither can I. At least not pictures. Not works of Art. I can paint furniture. And I can mend it. Luckily. Rather well. And yet. And yet. The Leonora sequence was very good. Fifteen of them. They sold. They were as I wanted them. I never touched Leonora. That was what made her so angry. It wasn't worship. Not impotence. It was – respect. That's what it was. Respect for an absolutely first class job done by Mother Nature. But underneath – O God.

Vicious. Vengeful. Vindictive.

When she couldn't destroy me she destroyed herself. How did she do it I wonder? We shall never know. Case closed. Person or persons unknown. But I think the police will always wonder about me.

I do myself sometimes. When I come down in the morning and find the place wrecked. Totally wrecked by me. Obviously by me. But I don't remember doing it. By my alter ego. Which Janice might like to know means other self. But the shrink said that manic-depressives are never schizophrenic. Unless he was having me on. Being kind to badly-damaged Patrick.

Janice is quite like Leonora. Same long legs. Same beautiful hands. Those hands have certainly seen life as you might say. I wonder if she knows what she really likes doing. But hands off is the rule. No sex. No co-habiting. Not even romantic walks in the garden. If you have to, go to the Library. Which is full of pornographic pin-ups supposed to turn you on. One day we'll find that Mona has defaced them. With the words These pictures degrade women. Which they do. Respect for the female body. Red-blooded men don't have it. So I'm queer. An old lush. Such a hopeless bloody failure that I can't even commit suicide properly.

Thank you.

Simon.

Dudley: But what I find hard to understand is how all you young people started off. In my generation we stayed at home too long. I accept that. Then we were pitch-forked straight into the war. But you, you young ones, never seem to have lived at home at all.

Janice: Depends what you mean by ome.

Mona: Dudley means a building lived in by both your parents at the same time where there is a room you can call your own.

Gerald: Very neat. J-just happens to be r-r-rubbish.

Clarissa: It just leaves out all the essentials.

Dudley: Which are?

Clarissa: Home is something which is part of you. And you are part of it. You belong to it and it belongs to you. Of course you share it with other people.

Layne: Yeh. I were in oner them once. Squattin we called it.

Mona: I think Clarissa meant that you shared it with people who loved you and whom you loved.

Dudley: Whom! Well done, Mona. Never thought I'd ever hear that word again.

Clarissa: Well I did and I didn't. There has to be one person to love. That is to say it makes it better if someone loves you, too. It's when someone you don't like comes in that the trouble starts.

Janice: Right, right. We was fine till my mum got married.

Layne: Wernt no women in the ome I were in.

Barry: Never did live with two parents. Me mum got done on a tombstone in Brompton Cemetery.

Sacred to er memory of Jeremiah something an is wife Adelaide. Polished marble. Showed it me once afore she scarpered.

Mona: Is it beginning to be a little clearer, Dudley?

Dudley: Yes. I'm afraid it is.

Mona: So if we're ever going to find out what sort of people we are, what sort of people we ought to be, we've got a lot of digging to do.

Gerald: D-digging? O God. Is th-that what we're all doing?

Mona: It's what I'm supposed to be doing. Helping you to find out who you are. I'm only just finding out about myself.

Gerald: B-b-best of British luck to you, M-Mona.

Clarissa: Of course, most of us haven't the faintest idea who we are. Or should that be whom? We've all been running away from ourselves for so long we can't remember who we were in the first place.

Mona: Perhaps I could help you find out?

Clarissa: Not sure I want to, thanks.

Gerald: C-c-couldn't f-face it?

Dudley: Very few of us could. But I suppose one has to stop running some time.

There is something very amiable about Dudley. He and I are the only two winos I think. Sometimes he looks like an Indian Army Colonel and sometimes he looks like a bundle of rags. For a man who can put away two bottles of sherry before breakfast, he looks remarkably fit. Who put him in here, I wonder? Not quite the Sludge of Society. I daresay we would recognise Clarissa's surname if we knew what it was.

Seem to have thought myself into a frightfully good temper. But we're all in the power of a sorcerer nevertheless. He isn't here but he's present. They. Would they send for the police if you scarpered, I wonder. Insane to talk about finding a reason for living. How can someone of Dudley's age, or anyone else for that matter, suddenly find a new reason for living? Like that wretched girl in the paper today. Forced to live by four judges. Poor little anorexic bitch. Compelled to live. Condemned to life.

That's what we all are. Condemned to live. But in recovery for the rest of our lives. As a picture framer. Don't think it ever occurred to my sainted brother that he was hitting me just about as hard as he could when he made me take that course. You're a good carpenter, he said. You understand about painting even if you can't do it. Or can't do it so that somebody wants it. Lucky he didn't turn me into an undertaker, I suppose. Though I might have liked that.

Producing really original coffins, coffins with integrity, coffins with a message. Being out on bail is no fun, if your brother is the bailee or whatever they're called. Coffins whose intellectual form bears no relation to their content. And all destined for the ultimate flames. Almost symbolic of one's life.

It's all very well to say that I don't know as much as Simon, which I don't. Compared to everyone else in this room I am Solomon himself. Solomon. Barry thinks he's a pawnbroker in Whitechapel. Janice and Layne have a client of that name who has to be cut in two without shedding one drop of Christian blood. The old girl stuck in the green chair knows who she is and so does Dudley. Mona too perhaps. Gerald thinks he's some sort of tycoon in the City. Darren doesn't think. And neither does this Charles Addams figure beside me on this sofa.

It is the most dangerous sofa I have ever sat on. A spring about to twang out and hit me on that sort of seam, where one's arse ends and one's balls begin. It looks as if someone has spilt Ribena all over this sofa, at specified intervals. A purple blodge, a yellow blodge, a green blodge, a brown blodge for God's sake. I hadn't noticed it before. And those dreadful blue wiggles. More phagocytes. They're the good ones, I remember now. Can't have too many phagocytes.

A very good idea about those coffins. I wonder where there is a coffin factory. But would they take me on with all my one-off ideas? At least Simon couldn't object to that. Always be a demand for coffins. Because there was nothing on those canvases. That was why I burnt them.

Clarissa: But don't you even know who your father was?

Layne: Nar, not much. Don't think me mum knew either.

Clarissa: But what does it say on your birth certificate?

Layne: My what?

Janice: Birth certificates is a middle-class luxury, Clarissa.

Clarissa: Didn't the hospital give you one?

Layne: Weren't born in ospital. It were a squat. Told you.

Clarissa: But – my God, that means you don't know who you are or even who you're meant to be. At least I know that.

Gerald: And who-who are you? Meant to. Be?

Clarissa: I am meant to be the daughter of my father by his legally married wife who ran off to Australia when I was twelve.

Gerald: Helluva lot that t-t-tells us.

Mona: It tells us that, at a most important time in her development, Clarissa had no one to advise her.

Clarissa: Do you always have to sound like a Government White Paper, Mona? Nobody ever talks like that. But you are right. Father was a stallion. Is a stallion. Different brood mare every week. Every day.

Gerald: D-d-dozens of l-little b-b-astard b-brothers and sisters?

Clarissa: No, he was too clever. Or the brood mares were.

Dudley: But who was this person who came to live in your house? The one you didn't like?

Clarissa: My mother came back.

Janice: Fightin, I bet.

Clarissa: Too right. I was the only thing left in her life that still belonged to her. And she was determined to keep it.

Mona: When was this?

Clarissa: I was seventeen.

Layne: An the kinky ole priest?

Clarissa: They sent me off to Switzerland to get a bit of peace.

III

JULIA

Gerald: D-diddn't d-divorce her then?
Clarissa: Never bothered. I was there when she came back. He just said Hallo you stringy old bitch. You can have the Yellow Room if you're staying. But you're not getting into my bed again.
Mona: And did she stay?
Clarissa: Yes. As far as I know she's still there. On the Patrick and Dudley circuit. I don't go.
Barry: So not avin parents is ard but avin em is arder.
Mona: All living is a problem. But once you've decided what the problem is it's easier to solve.
Patrick: Pin it down, you mean.
Layne: No, Patrick. No. No. No.
Janice: Sall right, Layne. E didn mean it.
Patrick: I did, as a matter of fact. I should think as much harm is done by clumsy helpers as was done in the first place.

Mona: I hope you're not talking about me, Patrick.

Patrick: No, Mona, I'm not. You're very good. Or almost. You don't push. You don't insist. I thought when I saw her first that Layne had that crushed look, as if she'd been in care all her life. Something about the way she walks.

Clarissa: You can tell about people from the way they walk?

Patrick: More than you might think. If you know what to look for.

Detached, yes, detached, that is what I feel, entirely detached from all these commonplace contentious people not exactly shouting at one another but getting quite excited and making such a noise that I cannot contemplate the events of last night in any sort of tranquility.

It is in any case impossible to contemplate anything on this murderous sofa, designed and made in sixteenth-century Spain to the specifications of Torquemada himself and washed ashore on the north coast of Cornwall as the Armada limped homewards.

Carelessly covered in a curtain material which was awarded a prize at the Festival of Britain in 1951 because it was even more hideous and brightly coloured than anything else at the time, the sofa is too large and too ugly for the discerning eye to be able to avoid it.

Unless of course one is sitting on it.

I am sitting on it. I sat on it yesterday but I am a different person today although the springs offer violence to both my buttocks in exactly the same way. And in the same places. They haven't changed at all in twenty-four hours but I must be a bit thinner than I was. After all that.

Everyone else in this room is trying to find a new life without something they had come to depend on, but I am supposed to be trying to find a new life with something that I had decided to do without.

What I would do in their position, by which I would be understood to mean the people who run this place and not the patients or that dreadful girl from Stockport, would be to make it very nice to look at, fill it with kind, comforting, helpful people and produce food that was fit to eat. For lunch, for instance.

How can they expect a person living with anorexia nervosa, as my ailment is so charmingly called, to consider, even for a moment, subjecting their digestive organs to one cubic inch of fish, boiled for a fortnight and shrouded in yellow sauce, the leg of a thin chicken similarly boiled and blanketed, along with everything else on the plate, in a white sauce, and a nameless unspecified pudding veiled in a pink sauce?

My digestive organs have been resting for too long to submit them to such a test, the poor darlings, and they reacted just as I expected them to. Sicked it all up without effort in the front hall. I wonder who is going to find it. Food is disgusting. We are disgusting, eating dead things in order to live. Killing living things in order to eat them in order to live. Who can justify their lives in terms of the thousands of living organisms they consume in a lifetime?

Don't be facetious, Julia. It isn't funny. Just rather silly.

A long silence in my mind. I have got to get my bearings again.

It is outrageous the way that woman's voice comes back to me when she has been dead for six weeks, that voice which has strait-jacketed me for nearly forty years. She has gone but the voice remains. Will always remain. I am here because it was a condition of her will. Dimly, dimly, I begin to discern that perhaps after all I do want to live. After last night, especially.

I must be very careful not to start talking aloud. I am not going to say anything today or any other day. That insane man who calls himself a psychiatrist told me yesterday that my condition could be treated but never cured and it could only be treated if I would co-operate. I think he actually thought that I was going to co-operate with him. If he seemed old to me, think how he must appear to those children opposite, all smoking their heads off. Not so much today. I suppose developing a new addiction is one way of getting rid of an old one. Replacement therapy I think they call it. One leg of mutton drives another down.

Neither am I going to listen to their conversation. All that talk about home. I heard that. I am closing my mind to them. I am closing my mind to their problems, their problems which apparently all have their roots in loveless uncared-for beginnings. How would they have got on with my life, over-loved, over-cared-for, over-protected, over-criticised, overborne, over-whelmed? Well may they ask who they are meant to be. I haven't the faintest idea who I am.

But.

I have done something.

I have performed a positive action. I must be very careful not to say a word. I am not going to say anything.

There is no one in this building with whom I could form even the most distant friendship. However highly qualified they all are, the staff here are simply doing a job. They do not get involved. They switch off at five. You have got to stop having problems until nine o'clock the next day. Except for Mona, of course. She is the link between old life and new life.

Do I need to enlarge any further on the state of our civilisation? There is the situation in a nutshell. Mona is the link. If there is no God, who is to save us?

Us, of course.

So Julia has taken Step One.

Of course it is rather ungracious to have these unchristian thoughts about Mona but really she is quite too perfectly awful. She means well. She means frightfully well. But it would take more than someone with her nonexistent qualifications, and her total lack of intelligence, imagination, intuition and information to be able to control, or benefit, this unbelievable collection of screwed-up personalities.

But she doesn't need to look so ghastly. Admittedly, God didn't give her much to work with, those froggy eyes. And those huge hands. And that bottom which seems to go right down to her knees. But if you have all these things you don't wear horn-rimmed spectacles or box-pleated tartan skirts badly in need of a jolly good clean. If your hands are huge you don't wave them about all the time. If your hair is nondescript at least you can wash it. But, you know, even if she did attend to all these things, she would still look like an ex-primary-school teacher from Stockport. Whatever they look like.

And how, one asks oneself, does an ex-primary-school teacher from Stockport acquire an expensive drug habit? Or even a cheap one? She's here because she's come through. Probably she went on one of those teachers' protest marches in the late seventies. All those crowds were rented, or hippies, or druggies who went along for the ride. Or the exercise. If it did happen like that, that is almost too awful to contemplate. I will try and be nice to Mona.

Always be careful what you wear, Julia. You're a very ugly little girl and we're the ones who have to look at you.

God, the way that voice comes back. Shall I ever get rid of it, I wonder?

Your mother is dead. My mother is dead. Mother is dead. Write it out a hundred times. Get it into your head.

Then coolly, calmly, collectedly, go through the events of the last year.

A year ago, not quite, my mother was informed that she was so riddled with cancer that there was nothing to be done. It came apparently out of a clear blue sky, no symptoms, no complaints. A routine check-up. She was told it would take about four months though it actually took eight. And she started confessing. There's something I must tell you, Julia. Your father was not my husband. He was a young cousin of my own.

I remember that cold hand in my bowel. How close, I asked. Not very close. A second cousin once removed. He was nineteen and I was thirty-nine. Yes, I said. Both at your sexual peak. Yes, she said. Did you ever see him again? O no. He went back to Canada. So he doesn't know? He doesn't know.

My husband left when you were born, as I've told you before. Yes, you have. Over and over again. As if being born were somehow my fault. We married just after the war, when we were all very anxious to get back to normal. And what is normal, I remember asking. The war had upset him a lot. He was a very nervous, sensitive man. He would have been a poet if he had had any talent. He made his career at the Arts Council. And of course he left when you were born as we had never had any sexual relations so you couldn't have been his.

That was how it all started. I couldn't face food. Either I just couldn't swallow it or I brought it up afterwards. I got thinner and thinner. And then she died. Leaving me all her property with an added codicil to the effect that it was conditional on my seeking treatment. I couldn't believe that was legal. But apparently it is. So here I am.

If you were not here, he still would be.

I must be perfect, I used to say to myself. I must be perfect to make up to Mother for the fact that she had no husband. I must be perfect to make her love me, to forgive me for being born. But no matter what I did, how many prizes I won at school, I could always have done better. The one thing she couldn't criticise was my scholarship to Somerville. She couldn't really even say that a scholarship to Lady Margaret, or to Girton or Newnham, would have been better.

And she followed me. That dreary little flat in Norham Gardens. We had coffee or lunch or tea together every single day. How, how, how did I ever endure it? I would have got a first if she hadn't been there. And it was a very good second. But the reproaches began. And have never stopped. Bonds of iron. Silver shackles. They should have dropped off automatically at the crematorium.

The house was always mine. She made it over. But how could I ever have guessed that she was sitting on nearly four million pounds? Have to give most of it to the Revenue of course, but still. On condition that I seek treatment. Of course the treatment only has to be sought. Doesn't have to be successful. I wonder who's going to find that ill-smelling mess in the hall.

I can't stand these thoughts another minute.
Let's see what's going on in Coronation Street.

Mona: But Layne, I don't understand. The police never had the power to clear squats, not unless you were trying to burn it down or something.
Layne: No, no, we wasn't. It were oner them council tower blocks. They was goin ter blow it up.
Mona: So that was when your – family – was broken up.
Layne: Fcourse, lookin at it now, I can't be sure the one I called Mum really was me mum. We was all shared, sort of.
Mona: Shared?
Layne: There was four kids in that squat. An two women. In our room, that is. Mum an Lena. There was more women afore that but they went.
Mona: Went where?
Layne: Sectioned off, probly. Passed on. They was all snortin or sniffin or somethin.
Mona: So then you were put into care. Are you ready to tell us about that?
Layne: No.
Janice: Your pushin er, Mona.
Patrick: And very hard. Do you remember how old you were, Layne? Or does it hurt too much?
Janice: Layne don't really know ow old she is, Patrick. We keep er birthday May the fourth

cos it sounds nice, like. But she don't know the year.

Layne: Bout eleven, I'd say. Big enough to get laid.

Clarissa: I agree, Layne. Men are disgusting.

Patrick: If being in care was anything like my schools it must have been dreadful. And no holidays. Worse than the squats I should think. So if you're seventeen now, you must have been in care for six years.

Layne: Oo says I'm seventeen?

Clarissa: He's just guessing, Layne. Patrick is a painter of the human female. He's having a good look at your tits.

Layne: Ow can e see em? Under all this.

Patrick: I have been thinking for some time, if you want to know, that Janice has a most beautiful body and you, what I can see of it, a very remarkable face.

Janice: Well thanks a bomb, Patrick.

Mona: Layne was only in care for three years. She told us that yesterday.

Layne: No, no, I never.

Mona: And you've known Janice for three years. So how did that happen?

Janice: We was on the road together.

Mona: If Layne was on the road, she must have been running away. Absconding.

Layne: No, no, I wernt.

Janice: Go on, tell er, luv. She can't do nothing. She's not the thorities an you never done nothing in the first place. Juss got sent to the wrong address.

Mona: She's right, you know, Layne. Get it off your chest. We're all on your side in here.

Layne: You got to prove that. Specially you.

Mona: Right. Before all these witnesses. Even if what you did was actionable, I wouldn't tell anyone. And neither would they. We're all trying to help.

Layne: Yer. Well. There's elp. And there's elp.

Janice: Go on, then. I'll old yer and.

Layne: Alright then. I did. I runned away fer the third ome I were in. Couldn take it no more. Jumped outer a winder. An ran.

Dudley: In my day you got a public thrashing for doing that. If they caught you.

A silence. A very silent silence. I apologise. Not Coronation Street at all. Thinking, feeling people. That poor old boy. Suddenly he looks about a hundred. But if that's what happened to him it must be more than fifty years ago. But one doesn't forget. So who's going to break the silence?

Gerald: G-going to tell us about it? Old ch-chap?

Of course. One should have known. There is something refreshingly bogus about Gerald. All the others have the air of being genuine even if they don't know who they are. But not Gerald. He comes out of an old film.

Janice: Come on, Uncle. Carin, sharin. If that's what appened to you you'll feel better if you tell us.
Dudley: Don't think you'll be interested. Long time ago.
Patrick: We would be. All of us.

He's not sure. He's looking round at us. Looking at me. What can I do? Smile? Yes, I can do that. And a little sort of bow of the head. Assent.

Dudley: Very well. It took place in the gym. The gymnasium, that is. There was a sort of dais at one end, with the wall bars behind it. The whole school was assembled by height, with the small ones in front, so that everyone could see. The headmaster explained that the penalty for running away was expulsion but that he had decided not to employ this extreme penalty. Then I was marched in, in my running shorts. Two of the prefects held my wrists over a vaulting horse. And the School Sergeant gave me seventeen cuts with a four foot cane. One for each year of my life.

Janice: Christ, Uncle. Where was this? Some kind of prison?

Dudley: It was a school, Janice. A very expensive boarding school. Costing my father a fortune.

Patrick: But you weren't really running away?

Dudley: No, I wasn't. That was the stupid thing. It was a dare.

Gerald: M-much more like it.

Dudley: In those days there were quite large blue enamel notices with white letters, saying: You may telephone from here. Stuck up above the phone boxes you understand. Well, on one of our longer runs, two of us saw one of these at the bottom of a stream. And he dared me to go and get it, add the words 'to God' after 'telephone' and nail it on the chapel door. Sounded like good clean fun. So I set off, fully clothed, in the middle of the night. But two of the masters, coming back from some late night binge, saw me. About three miles from the school. So of course they thought I was running away. And as I hadn't got the blinding notice, it was a bit awkward.

Patrick: But didn't he come forward? The one who dared you, I mean.

Dudley: No, he didn't.

Patrick: A shit.

Dudley: Yes. He later had a successful career in politics.

Mona: And what did it do to you, the physical experience? With hindsight.

Dudley: It taught me to hate. To hate any man more than fifteen years older than I. And never to trust anyone again. Of course in some ways I was lucky. I had already got entrance to Sandhurst. Expulsion would have cancelled that. And to give him his due, the School Sergeant tried to apologise to me afterwards. Said he was only obeying orders. What I now call the Nuremburg Excuse. But I couldn't speak to him, or anyone else. And I left at the end of the term.

Patrick: And after Sandhurst? If you survived it?

Dudley: Went into the Gurkhas. Had a very good war.

Barry: Wots the gurkers then? Sounds like a lotter bollocks to me.

Dudley: They come from Nepal. Fantastic fighters. In the days of the British Empire they could be relied on absolutely. True as steel. Completely loyal.

Janice: Never eard of a British Empire. I knows the one in Leicester Square ercourse.

Gerald: And the one-one that f-fought back.

Janice: Did we really ave a British Empire, then? One of our very own?

Dudley: I hardly think this is the time for a history lesson.

And suddenly Dudley is somebody else. He is sitting more upright. No longer a heap of assorted rags. You can see that he was an Army Officer, that he did have a very good war, that perhaps his men really would have followed him, if not to the end of the earth at least as far as Rangoon. But the young ones seem to know nothing, not the Empire, probably not the war. If my mother hadn't talked about it all the time – and if she hadn't been so old – I daresay I would never have heard of it either.

So I'm not the only one in this room to have had a privileged upbringing. Patrick, certainly, Gerald much less certainly. A very minor public school if it was one. Amazing to think that Dudley's father paid – I wonder what it was then – about eighty pounds a term to have him treated like that. And that is what the trendies call a privileged upbringing. Still, compared to what Layne, and probably Janice, have gone through, I suppose it was.

I am getting very excited. I shall start talking if I'm not careful.

I must sit still. I don't feel as if my arms were going to drop off as I did last week. Had to hug them very close to me because I can't do without my arms. Of course last week I was rather hoping to die, without any effort on my part I mean. Just quietly melt away. Dudley is melting now, subsiding into his clothes again. His moment has passed. I don't think he got those clothes from Oxfam. Macmillan Cancer or the Distressed Gentlefolk I should think. But rather a long time ago. I am putting off my own moment.

I know that. It's not that I don't want to face it, because after what happened last night I know that I can face it, that I can face very nearly anything. Alone. That is the secret. I must be alone. Surrounded if you like by well-wishers, but if I am ever going to achieve anything I have to do it by myself. Of course that voice will always be there but I must talk back at it. I have to say Mother your cruelty and selfishness almost pass belief. What a mess you made of the excellent material you gave birth to. I should have said that twenty years ago. But I didn't.

So let us, in a very detached and rational manner, consider the events of last night.

Deep breath. Hold it, but not for too long. Breathe out.

I did not jump out of the window like Layne. I walked out of the French windows in this room which are closed by a catch which would not defeat even the most amateur burglar.

I was wearing the Maltese nightdress, hand-embroidered by some genius on Gozo and large enough to reveal absolutely nothing. I didn't want it to look like a sex murder. And the pink dressing gown from Harvey Nichols which was rather a mistake as it was much too pale. And my slippers of course. Gliding through beechwoods in bare feet would have been much too painful. Dead beech nuts are sharp. And noisy. All those twigs. I couldn't believe that my progress through the wood wouldn't be heard by someone. But it wasn't. I made quite sure, several times, that I wasn't being followed.

I had heard this train every night. Every night it passed at exactly half past one. I cannot think where it was going to, Penzance perhaps, but as it always came at the same time I supposed it was a passenger train. And it always seemed to go very quickly, passing in a matter of seconds.

Extraordinary the amount of trouble they go to to prevent people getting on to railway lines. As if they had a serious problem with would-be suicides in this remote corner of Wiltshire. Who on earth ever thought of building this startlingly unlovely residence in this ravishingly beautiful position? A Bristol merchant, they say, but it is too young to have been built with slave money. Though it is haunted, no doubt about that, house and woods, and by women. There were a lot of surplus females in the 1880s. And then to call it Copsewood as if it were a villa at the end of some suburban avenue.

So there I was on the railway line. I found a gap in the brambles in the end but there was still rather a lot of barbed wire. However, one's ballet training came in useful. I am quite sure Mother never thought of that. It was a long straight section going into a tunnel with woods on both sides. That was why the noise didn't last long. And then I started wondering what to do.

Lady Jane Grey and Mary, Queen of Scots, had their hair cut off – and, of course, not very much choice. Gloria Swanson was always tied to the track which would have made the most fearful mess except that the train always stopped in time. Or the hero arrived. I decided, like Charles the First, to lay my head on the track, down, as upon a bed.

But that cold steel on my throat was a shock, though of course as I lay there for some time it got warmer. The steel I mean. And I put my hair up away from my neck although I don't think an express train is quite the same as an axe. And lay there. I had left fifteen minutes to get on to the line as I didn't want to have time to re-consider. It should have been on me in a moment.

I don't know how long it was. Naturally I hadn't brought my watch. But it seemed a very long time. I wondered if I was on the up line and not on the down one. And then I remembered it was Sunday. The time would be different. Or perhaps it wouldn't come at all. And I sat up, furious at my own stupidity and forgetfulness.

And there it was. You would think a train like that would make more noise and it was coming very fast. And suddenly I knew I couldn't. I should have rolled down the bank but I wasn't quick-witted enough. I lay down beside the track to avoid the slipstream, but there was a long strand of hair over the rail and I didn't dare to move, clinging on to a sleeper with my hand, my left one luckily. All my nails are broken. And the wheels kept saying 'You don't want to live but you don't want to die, You don't want to live but you don't want to die'. And then it went. Unbelievably quickly.

I lay a moment to give all that air time to settle and then I ran. Stupidly sobbing. I could hear the train slowing.

They must have seen me. And I ran as fast as I could, realising that the one thing I was afraid of was being caught. I couldn't face the explanations. I found a gap, bigger than the other. There was an old moon, lying on its back. I ran through the wood. That was when I felt those ghosts. I was in the house before the train came back. I heard some talking but no shouting. And everyone in Copsewood slumbered on as if nothing had happened.

But it took me ages to get to sleep.

Clarissa: But you didn't have to go through all that by yourselves. You could have gone to a doctor.

Janice: Clarissa, I keep tellin you. People like Layne an me isn't real people, with documents an things. You as to register with a doctor. You as to be on is list. I'm a bit more real an Layne, I spose, as I were born in ospital. But nobody knows Layne exists.

Clarissa: Except the people at those homes.

Janice: Well, she were on their books I spose. But if she wanted a passport she couldn get one. You as to ave the proper piecer paper.

Clarissa: But they could see she exists, couldn't they? If she went.

Layne: Nar. They'd juss say can't find no proofer your existence. Madam proberly. The evidence of my eyes is not sufficient. What e used to say, remember Janice, that one with the kink about the Revenue.

Janice: But it were OK in the end. Not a miscarriage. Juss a missterious miss. We was a bit sad after all.

Clarissa: But could you have kept a baby? Poor little thing.

Janice: No we couldn, not where we were. But it would ave put us on the ousing list.

Mona: Except that it would probably have been born with your addiction and you might not have liked that.

Patrick: I don't know. Going through life on Cloud Nine right from the beginning might be rather nice. Cushioned against reality as you might say.

Gerald: R-r-right. Reality is the p-p-problem.

Mona: And we're all here to help each other cope with it.

Clarissa: You are marvellous, Mona. No argument. Bright. Breezy. Both feet on the ground.

Mona: Well, someone has to keep them there. Just to remind us what we are doing here.

Patrick: At the moment we are forming an admiration society aimed at Janice and Layne. Because for guts and stamina, as they used to be called, they really deserve a prize. I envy their will to live.

Clarissa: And yet you probably have more reason for living than anyone else in this room. If you'd just admit it.

Patrick: Which is what?

Clarissa: Patrick, I saw those paintings. They were fantastic. So all right, I was supposed to be admiring Batholomew's black daubs, but all I could see were those glowing pictures of that wonderful red girl. Why don't you tell us about her?

Patrick: Pushing, Clarissa?

Clarissa: Yes, Patrick. Pushing.

Patrick: Well, she came to a bad end. But not at my hands.

Gerald: How c-can you know that?

Barry: Cos e didn go roun stoned outer is mind on acid days an weeks atter time. Is blinds ony went on a few days. Ours maybe. Right, Patrick?

Patrick: Right, Barry. And I never went out.

Gerald: C-c-can't understand why B-b-barry knows so m-m-much about me.

Barry: Cos I been there too ercourse. We was at that party. Told yer. Remembers you perfick. Couldn make out if you was trying to top yourself or your mate.

Gerald: Wh-what did he l-l-ook like?

Barry: You. Two peas in a pod.

Gerald: O G-G-God. T-t-trevor. What th-then?

Barry: An then the perlice arrives, din they?

So Gerald has lost his memory. How I envy him. His mind, too, if he had one. Frightening how the past hangs over one, like a dark cloud. Or clings like a back pack. And we all have one, all trying to get away from it. What they all must be going through I am thankful I can't imagine, withdrawal symptoms and everything. And no drink. No medication of any kind. So not surprising if they're all off their heads a bit. My dreams are terrifying enough. Theirs must be much worse.

It is very untranquil, their conversation. I think I have heard enough for one day, though it is more interesting than one might have thought. They really all are in the same boat, though for different reasons. Perhaps this is the classless society at work. They all have the same living conditions. We all have the same living conditions. I suppose, if they leave me any of Mother's money, I could offer a home to Janice and Layne. But of course it's love, not money, that they need. Well so does everyone of course. But if I were to offer that, wouldn't I be trying to possess them? It would be Mother and me all over again.

Life in the Museum is calm. The prints don't criticise, or argue, or sulk, or burst into tears. They are safe. I am safe. Life doesn't intrude. But here I am surrounded by it and this is a completely new experience for me and one that I don't like very much. I really must change my position. Both my buttocks have gone to sleep. Perhaps if I don't move the paralysis will spread. Slow starvation is not violence. Total paralysis wouldn't be violence. So I won't move.

What a very strange idea to put that very nasty seventies wallpaper above the spinach green lincrusta. What would you think the designer had in mind, a block of spinach green, a block of cabbage green, a block of lettuce green, and then a block of beetroot? Perhaps he began life in some kind of institutional kitchen. Which reminds me that I had hoped to keep down my horrid lunch. If you make up your mind to go on living, your troubles are supposed to be over. Of course it was pretty disgusting but it will be very awkward if my stomach has developed an antipathy to food. To that food, anyhow.

Perhaps I should offer to go and work in the kitchens and cook something for myself that I am actually able to eat. Well, what a brilliant idea. And then a book. *Alimentation for Anorexics*. There would be no words in it at all and we would all make a fortune. Especially the printer. And so if I brought up that lunch it must mean that I haven't made up my mind to go on living. Curious the fuss they make if you die when they don't seem to mind what your life is like so long as you're actually breathing. But that book is a marvellous idea. I must remember not to tell anyone.

Dudley is quite silent. Poor old boy. He must have been incredibly handsome when he was young. For a moment one could see it, the glorious young officer swinging through the trees of the Burmese jungle. Or whatever they did. Now he's just a tired and sad old man almost indistinguishable from his thick-knit oatmeal pullover. He must be boiled. And all because he told us something he has probably never told anyone before.

The penny drops. That, my dear Julia, is what you have got to do. Share. You have to sick it all on to them. You have to tell Layne how lucky she was not to have had a mother. There isn't any point in sitting here thinking it over. I hope I haven't been talking it all over. I think they would have mentioned it. And there isn't anyone in the room who would understand my little problem. Except Mona perhaps. And O dear the ignominy of being understood by Mona. I don't think I could stand that.

Perhaps it would be easier to die after all.

But quietly. No more railway trains.

Do be careful, Julia. You're all I have.

All right, Mother.

All right.

But, my God, if I do let myself die I shall be re-joining Mother. Either up there or down there. And I've only just got rid of her.

I'd better start playing their game.

Clarissa: Gerald, why don't you just shut up and let Barry tell us all what happened as he obviously knows and you don't. Your questions are getting us nowhere.

Gerald: OK then. B-b-barry, please.

Barry: Right frer the start then.

Janice: There were this old mansion, right? Stuck in the middler nowhere, right? And you was avin this festival, right? Raisin money for charity, right?

Layne: An you was all as igh as bloody kites on bloody acid, right.

Mona: Yes, thank you, Janice and Layne. We've all got that. Start from where the police arrived, please, Barry.

Barry: Right. Then the pigs arrived, right?

Janice: Right.

Layne: Right.

Clarissa: Too right.

Barry: My gaffers scarpered. Organisers, right? But I didn. Didn ave nothin on me so they couldn pin nothin. But I were stoned right outer me mind an kicked a coupla pigs where it urts most so they took me in, right?

Gerald: And k-k-kicked you where it hurts m-m-most.

Barry: Nar, they was as good as gold. Magistrits an that. Remanded. On bail.

Gerald: Where did you g-g-get that?

Clarissa: Gerald, what planet are you living on? Anyone would think you'd just come out of the schoolroom. His gaffers put it up of course.

Barry: On condition I come ere.

Gerald: So. G-got that. B-b-but how long ago was all th-this?

Barry: Party were Forther July. Dependence Day, right? My gaffers as a funny senser umour.

IV

GERALD

Gerald: And h-h-how long ago is that?
Mona: Two months, Gerald. All but a few days.
Gerald: Ch-Ch-Christ. Where've I been for two m-months?
Mona: Perhaps I can help you there. The full name of this establishment is the Copsewood Detoxification Unit. It is privately run but of course it accepts referrals from juvenile courts and probation officers. And higher courts too, sometimes.
Gerald: N-now we get there. Is that m-me?
Mona: Yes. But it's nothing to worry about.
Gerald: B-but wh-what am I charged with? N-n-not illegal to go to. P-p-parties.
Mona: Fraud, as I understand. And the police are anxious to trace your partner.
Gerald: O G-God. Have they found him?

Mona: Not to my knowledge. You know the problems with country police forces. This is Wiltshire but the offences seem to have been committed in Lancashire.

Gerald: W-w-wish I could th-think straight.

Barry: If you was usin the stuff my gaffers was sellin you probly won't never think straight again.

Gerald: B-b-but. I m-must be on b-b-bail.

Mona: Yes. Your wife, I understand.

Gerald: M-m-my w-wife? And who-who the h-hell is she?

Mona: Well, you know, Gerald, that is the kind of thing you ought to be able to tell us.

Barry: Looks like someone kicked Gerald juss where it urts most.

Patrick: I know how you feel, Gerald. Lean back in your chair, breathe deeply and count up to five hundred.

Gerald: J-j-just tell me th-this. Wh-where did I c-come from?

Mona: That we don't know. I should take Patrick's advice if I were you.

Gerald: B-b-bloody well w-wish you were me.

Not a dream. Bloody well wasn't a bloody dream. At least I can think straight. A bit. Mind isn't stammering. Just blank. That ignorant flea-ridden whore must have married me. Gave her power of. Atrophy I shouldn't wonder. A joke. What a load of bloody trouble she's saddled herself with. So that crappy old bloke leering at me was real. God his breath was thick. Can still smell it. And his teeth enormous. And somebody saying Say Si, Senor, say Si, Senor. So I said it. God, I was getting married. Only hope it was Gabriella and not that lousy little Fernanda. Lean and hungry. Tiny tits. Biggest pussy I've ever been in. Jaws. Eat you up if she could. But I don't remember her teeth. They could be hers, the ones which come at me, chomp, chomp, chomp, out of the darkness. Snakes growing out of the gums. And then that tongue. Wipes it all off. Bursts into flames. That's a dream. Has to be a dream. God how I wish it would stop.

Two months. Two bloody months. What've I been doing all that time? Don't even forget getting here. Remember. Don't remember anything. A hole. Trevor in it. Remember him. And the wood with the black figures digging. Is that what we're meant to be doing here? And the lights. White lights not blue lights. Not the pigs. Is it real? The flames? All my dreams finish up in flames. Must be a dream then. Burning. Some dreams and some not dreams.

Gabriella would be OK. Soft. Comfortable. Bones grind together with Fernanda. That's what happens when you have arth. Arth. Gone. Prefers sitting on me anyway. If I can remember that it's something. Ritis. Been talking all the afternoon. Taking part. Putting a good face on. Think I have. Got to do that.

Very dark last night. Woke up. Something seemed to click on. Or off. As if I'd been switched on. Wires crossed. Uncrossed. Lay there and there was someone else in the room. Not snoring. Just grunting. A man. A train passed. Long way off. And came back with loud talking. Not shouting. Went away again. Where am I? Who am I? Lay in a muck sweat wondering. Who's this person. Couldn't remember my own name. All call me Gerald here. Perfectly good name. Just don't think it's mine. That's all.

Patrick: That's better, Gerald. The ghost has walked over your grave and gone away. Amazing how long it takes to count up to five hundred.

Gerald: J-j-just tell me th-this. How l-long've I been here?

Patrick: The same time as all the rest of us. Nine days. This is our eighth meeting.

Gerald: And I've been to all the m-meetings?

Patrick: So far as I remember.

Gerald: D-don't remember this r-room before.

Patrick: A difficult room to forget.

Mona: Yes, you have, Gerald. But this is the first time we've been able to understand you.

Clarissa: Absolute rubbish was your speciality. Interesting, of course. Illuminating in some ways. But serious rubbish.

Janice: Barry were the one oo splained what you was sayin. Seemed to know all about you.

Gerald: P-perhaps he could s-splain to me?
Barry: Only guessin mind. But you was wunner my gaffers' runners.You an that bloke. Twins you mighter been. Only blokes with ties at the festival which is why I remembers. You scarpered. An the other bloke. An me gaffers ercourse.
Gerald: And w-what were we p-pushing? Th-that's what runners do isn't it? E-especially?
Barry: Especially ecstasy. But there were another kind more expensive called igh ecstasy. Very pricey. Not too many customers but all very posh. So the gaffers needed a posh salesman.
Gerald: Ecst. Ecstasy I know. A-acid and amphet. But high ecstasy? Amphetamines.
Barry: Reckon there were a touch of smack included. Never tried myself.
Gerald: Ch-Ch-Christ. If I w-was on th-that I'm l-lucky to be alive. If it is l-l-lucky. If I. Am.
Mona: You're moving much better today. You were a bit creaky before. It's only your mind that's likely to be permanently affected.
Gerald: W-well, th-thanks a m-million, M-mona. M-makes me f-feel much. B-b-better.
Mona: No point in concealing the facts. That's what we've been doing. Now we have to face them. Head on.
Barry: If you was on igh ecstasy all them two months, or even ornery ecstasy, you wouldn

remember nothin. Likely that were what the gaffers wanted.

Gerald: Why-why-why would they? W-want that?

Barry: Wouldn want you in er witness box shootin yer mouth orf would they?

Gerald: So I'm w-w-wanted. Drug Squad. F-f-fraud Squad. What's to stop me r-running away?

Mona: Nothing. No fences. But you have no money and we'd have to let them know.

Gerald: How does B-b-barry know so m-much?

Mona: Caught in the same net.

Clarissa: Dredged.

Nothing. Darkness. Nothing. Close my eyes and there are the flames. Flames and snakes and teeth. Won't close them. Keep them open and look around. Get my. Bloody uncomfortable chair. Why can I remember Fernanda and Gabriella and nothing else? Bearings. That's what they are. Someone been feeding me this stuff. Reduce the dose when they wanted me. Up-up-something. Upright. Able to say Si Senor. Gabriella Colombia. Fernanda Brazil. I'm foreign. Might be very useful. But why do I know this. Nothing else. Where did it happen? And why fraud?

No point in asking. I can't answer. Load of scarecrows in this room. Bag of old female bones on the sofa. Black hair. Black dress. Can't see her face. Must have one. Patrick not a bag of bones. Fifty. Looks like a. Gone. That word. I had it. Gone. Animal that comes out at night. Lives in a hole in the ground. Fat old girl in the tub chair, sound asleep. Gave up trying to talk. Words came out all wrong. Like mine. All right but a stammer. Meaning's OK. Can't find that animal. Mona. Could anyone fancy Mona? John Thomas sound asleep. My room-mate wanking himself silly this morning. Went on pretending to be asleep. What a racket when he came. Thought he was going to die. Barry. I'll have to ask him. Ask him what? What he thinks of when he's wanking. Not what I meant.

Pushers don't get had for fraud. Get charged with pushing.

Barry's wearing grey trousers and grey shoes. I'm wearing grey trousers and grey shoes. The winos have got sneakers. No laces. Barry and I have the same shirt. Christ, we're in uniform.

Gerald: But th-th-this isn't a remand home.

Mona: No, it isn't. I've already told you. It's a detoxification centre. Please stick to the point.

Gerald: Wh-what's that?

Mona: The point? or the place?

Gerald: P-p-place.

Mona: It's a place where people come to get the poisons out of their systems. You're only just beginning.

Gerald: F-f-feels like H-h-hell to me.

Layne: O no. Ell is where we've come from. Not like this. Very nice ere.

Mona: Can we get back to our discussion?
Gerald: S-sorry. Didn't m-mean to interrupt.
Mona: You didn't know you were talking aloud, did you?

Better not answer. Didn't. Back to the flames again. Keep your eyes open. Keep my eyes open. Can't relax in this chair. Didn't know you had bones in your arse. Perhaps I should look into the flames. See what I can see? O Christ. It's the teeth again. With snakes. They must be somebody's teeth. No one could have teeth that big. The snakes are green today. Black yesterday. Patterns on. And teeth. Never knew snakes had teeth. Open your eyes. Open your eyes.

Those little bimbos in the armchair must be very thin. Seem to have plenty of room. Both in black tights. Mini dresses I suppose. Layne in a long T-shirt. No face either. Both a bit green still. Clarissa looks OK. One very high-class bird. Got the best chair. Biggest anyway. Not on the game. Not on any game. What's she doing here? No one's good enough for her. Bright though. Ripe though. Not really asking for it. You'd be wrong. Little black slug on the window seat. Hasn't said anything. No name. If he is a he. Hard to tell sometimes. I've been here seven times before. Can't remember them.

What can I remember with my eyes open?

Gerald. No surname. Trevor really. God yes, I think I am. I've been switched. The gaffers have switched me.

Someone else. Clever. The black figures were burying Gerald. Settle for that anyway. But the lights? White lights. Pigs' lights are blue. Even grotty little provincial pigs have blue lights. PC Plod. Middle of a wood. Except I think they were digging something up.

So Barry says. A runner. Posh salesman. And all those words. Smack and coke and acid and crack and dope. And track marks for Christ sake. Track marks. Someone else did it if I have. And I have. No wonder I can't remember. Anything. But I can speak. I know the words. I understand what they say. But the big hole. Like a wiped-out.

Commuter.

That's a very good. Allergy. Anatomy. Anthology. I know a lot of words still. Not the one I want. You can wipe off a commuter's memory and still leave it able to work. Computer. That's what they've done. To me. Hands in my gut are back. Cold hard hands. Clamping. Cramping. Sit still. O God the pain. My feet are made of lead. Keep them still too. Breathe. Breathe. Relax. They've got you. I can't. But I can go on breathing.

Shouldn't have closed my eyes. All still here. Big black hands now. Some with knives. Mustn't scream. Flames and snakes and teeth. And the tongue. What the hell is it doing? Licking everything clean? Cloth on a windscreen. But all the shit comes back again. Sell my soul for a glass of water.

Haven't got a soul. Sold it. Beginning to go soggy.

Janice: Don't agree completely. If what you're doin is survivin you can't be that fussy.
Dudley: But you must know the difference between right and wrong.
Janice: Can't say as I do. Not always. What is it?
Dudley: O my God.
Patrick: He needs notice of that question.
Barry: Fyou gets nicked it's wrong. Fyou don't it's OK.
Mona: But that's not what they taught you at school.
Barry: Wot you mean – school?
Mona: Didn't you go to school?
Barry: O yer, we all went. Even Layne an Darren proberly went. But didn learn nothin.
Layne: No I never. Not a school where you ad lessons. In a classroom. That right, Patrick? Classroom.
Patrick: Quite right. But what about that home you were in?You must have had some lessons there.
Layne: Well, yer. Not what you'd call school lessons. More ow ter clean windows an scrub floors. Didn ave no books.
Dudley: Don't tell us you were sewing mailbags.
Layne: No we wasn't sewin. Wasn really doin nothin. There were a telly an a radio. An exercise. An workin in the kitchen.
Mona: So you can cook?

Layne: Well, not exackly cook. I can peel spuds with me eyes shut.

Mona: That's something, I suppose.

Janice: Yer, somethin. It don't take three years to learn ter peeler potater. Layne's bright. Got a brain. Juss never been allowed ter use it.

Julia: Perhaps I could help.

Mona: I didn't quite catch that. Julia, very nice to hear from you. I expect your voice is a bit rusty.

Julia: I said perhaps I could help.

Janice: Thought you was asleep.

Julia: We look for a middle way. I've had too much education. You've had too little. You don't have to say anything now, but I could help you with your reading and writing. If you wanted me to.

Barry: An what about me?

Patrick: I think we should wait until Julia's a bit stronger before she takes you on.

Barry: Don't slappem aller time. An only the awkward ones then. Can be as gentle as a little lamb. Tell you later.

Dudley: Public education has been free and compulsory since 1870, not 1970. The schools are there. They have been for over a century. You just have to go there.

Clarissa: The thing is, Uncle – and I'm only just beginning to understand this – if you have no documents – and Layne has no documents, you don't have to do anything. You don't exist. So you don't go to school. And there's no one to see that you do.

Dudley: There were in my day.

Mona: Well yes, there were. But then in those days people led more settled lives. The inspectors knew where everyone was so they could make sure the children were at school. But that's impossible now, especially in somewhere like London.

Dudley: They could do it if they had a little more gumption.

Barry: Don't know what that is exackly. But I'd like ter see you inspectin the kinder squat Layne were in. Was in one meself once. Can still smell it sometimes.

Patrick: Well, tell us about it.

Barry: It wernt a squat proper. Four on us, on security. Empty council flat but we wasn't paying nothin cos it were Lambeth. Reckon everyone in the ole block were on giro. Fridays it usually came. Then it started to come Saturdays. Then Mondays. So what did they do? Kidnapped the poor bloody postman an eld im to ransom. I scarpered. Stinked of real trouble.

Dudley: So you do know the difference?

Barry: Sometimes you could say. But not so's I could sit on a jury.

Dudley: You hardly look old enough.

Barry: Twenty-two. Ole chap.
Mona: The judge usually tells you what to do.
Janice: So where's the point of the jury then?
Barry: Wouldn mine a bitter jury. Might get Gerald off of the ook on is.
Patrick: And I bet you would too.

Very kind of Barry. Not much point in talking. Good to have a friend. Think he's going to need a friend on the jury too. What's he mean by a tax man? A mob, Janice said. Right on. Probably. And all this talk about school. Can't remember school. Must've been there. I talk proper. But its name. Where it was. Can't. Try not to panic. Losing your memory's not like losing your mind. Mind's still here. Just got nothing in it. Wiped clean. Re-pro. Pro. But I can remember Gabriella and Fernanda. Grammed. Very strange. And that other thing. Power of? Something. Analogy. That's it. Patrick looks like a beaver.

No. No he doesn't. Wrong word still. Slobbering a bit. Don't seem to have a handkerchief. Have to be back of my hand. Got to keep my eyes open and my mouth shut. Still can't see through the flames. Black figures. Coming for me. Mustn't scream. Running. Through the wood. What were they doing? Never know that. Don't want to. Don't want to know anything. Want to sit here for ever. Safe. Well. Quite safe. Couldn't get out even if I did want to. My legs don't work. No money. Wouldn't think there's even anything to steal in this place.

One thing I want to know. The fraud. Don't think I'm clever enough to carry off a good fraud. Wouldn't be here if I had. Been caught all along the line. Mona might know. Do I want to know? Really. Can't close my eyes as it is. Can't really sleep. Seems to be a metal. In my stomach. What are they called? O God. Another word gone. Turn something. Turnstile. That's better. Going slowly round and round. The black hands are still there. Behind the flames. And the teeth. And the tongue. And the snakes. Break it. Break it. Break it.

Gerald: M-mona?
Mona: Yes, Gerald. Just a minute.
Janice: It's OK. Not important. See what e wants.
Mona: Now Gerald.
Gerald: Wh-what do you know about the F-fraud Squad?
Mona: You mean, do I know what you're supposed to have done?
Gerald: Y-y-yes. I mean that.
Mona: You and your partner are supposed to have sold off an entire block of holiday flats in Torremolinos knowing that it had already been demolished.
Barry: An where's the arm in that? Good scam.
Mona: Scams are not good, Barry.
Gerald: And th-th-that's all?
Mona: Enough I would have thought.

Gerald: D-doesn't seem v-very serious. Wh-who-who got hurt?

Mona: The purchasers, Gerald. Twenty flats at fifty thousand a time is a million pounds.

Gerald: And I've g-got that?

Mona: That's what the Fraud Squad wants to know.

Gerald: Wh-what else do you kn-know about me?

Mona: Very well. You come from Croydon. Privately educated until expelled from school for drug abuse. Disappeared completely – that is to say, nothing is known – until you were found a fortnight ago unconscious in a hotel in Bloomsbury with fifteen thousand pounds worth of heroin in your sponge bag. Your papers were in order and genuine. So they were able to trace you back.

Gerald: P-p-parents? You t-told me about my w-w-wife.

Mona: No parents. At least, they've moved. The present owner at the address on your passport application didn't know where they were. But they had lived there all right.

Gerald: Ch-Christ. Well, th-thanks, Mona.

Deeper and deeper. Shouldn't have asked. Croydon. Where's that? I mean I know but I'm sure I never lived there. So. Lean back and think of Croydon. O God those hands. They'll get me. Don't lean back. The knives are out. Never be able to sleep again. The place I lived in began with a B. B for Beaver. Patrick does not look like a beaver. Looks like a badger. Got it. Badger. He doesn't look like a badger. Not grey enough. Patrick looks like a – banker. Another B. Banker de Something. O Christ yes. Banco de somewhere. That woman's voice. Lembra sempre. Something like that. Banco de. O God. I can't remember. But you used to live in Bedford. Bedford. Yes. Bedford. Barry said Trevor was very like me. He was. They have switched us. Gerald is dead and now I'm Gerald. I suppose I've got his passport. Pigs must have it. Like to know how old I am. Surname. That sort of thing. Essential part of a. Of course the fuzz have got that passport. Where's my actual one do you think? A gentleman's education. Never see it again. Nowhere to hide. Not even in my head. Only distraction. Listen to the discussion group. Discussion and distraction. Very good. But a something for despair.

Blueprint. Another B. B for blueprint.

A blueprint for despair. And B is for Bird.

Julia: No, I meant this. If nothing is ever taught in our schools – at least not in the ones we're talking about – it stands to reason that nothing is ever learnt.

Dudley: But you can't go to school for eleven years without something sinking in.

Barry: Yer. You can. Easy.

Julia: The right to be educated presupposes the right not to be educated. The right to live presupposes the right to die. The right to create presupposes the right to destroy.

Patrick: What kind of logic is that?

Julia: Anorexic logic if you like. You had the right to destroy your paintings, didn't you? I was listening, you know. You destroyed what you had created.

Patrick: Right. I had that right. What I thought we were talking about was the right to destroy something that someone else had created. Before all this talk about school.

Julia: Meaning a self, I suppose? As the creation of a man and a woman we are sacred, is that what you mean? Without the right to destroy ourselves?

Janice: Sacred? What utter bleedin rubbish. Sacred! Layne were made during a gang-bang. Er mum didn ave a clue which one it were. Barry came from a one-night stand on a tombstone.

Barry: Nar. It were in the lunchour, me mum said.

Janice: OK. An my mum said she were pretty sure it were the postman but couldn promise. An Darren juss grew. Under a stone.

Mona: But once you are alive, no matter how you come alive, then your life is sacred. I think, Julia?

Janice: Sacred to oom? See, Uncle, I'm a quick learner.

Dudley: I had noticed. And sacred to yourself, Janice. Though I quite see it's very easy to forget that.

Barry: Bloody easy if you never knowed it in the first place.
Janice: Well roger me rigid. Been sacred all this time and nobody never told me.
Patrick: So we're telling you now.
Clarissa: But if these brilliantly creative people forfeit their rights in you as their possession – for some reason or for no reason – what then? Whom do you belong to?
Dudley: Perhaps I should have been an English teacher after all.
Patrick: You are your own unencumbered property, Clarissa. And you are quite right, of course. Procreation is about the only creative activity available to ninety-nine per cent of the population.
Dudley: Quite so. We are already a nation of voyeurs.
Layne: You can say that again.
Janice: Onlooker sees the bester the game.
Mona: The onlooker sees most of the game. Not the same thing.
Janice: Right, right. An gawpin on the sidelines is borin.
Julia: Exactly. Boredom is the great enemy. If you don't understand a civilisation, you can't appreciate it. Half of us, more than half I rather think, spend our days in a thick fog of bored non-comprehension. So we take to drugs, drink,

food, gang-bangs, tombstones. All because we can't think of anything better to do.

Patrick: And if we can think of something better to do and then find we can't do it?

Julia: Another ball-game altogether. Everyone can do something. I don't mean to say that everyone can do something well, but that isn't the point.

Janice: So what can our Barry aksherly do, then?

Barry: One thing anyow. Or I could. Seems to ave died on me.

Dudley: It's the saltpetre in the tea.

Julia: What else can you do, Barry?

Barry: Well, I suppose. Paintin. Not pictures. Doors an that.

Patrick: What colour would you paint this room?

Barry: The Green Room, right? So it as ter be green. But them doors don't ave ter be that ackshle shade of cabbage. There were a name I learned this mornin. Owe de somethin. Pale. Bitter grey. If you done all the dark green lighter, winders an all that stuff at the bottom, wouldn be so grotty. Make the other colours brigher like.

Dudley: Lincrusta. You have to be my age to know that.

Patrick: I quite agree. Let's hope you have a great future.

Barry: Yer. Right.

Mona: And where were you this morning?

Barry: Tell you later, Mona. Got it all worked out.

Julia: Always nice to have one's theories confirmed. And so quickly too. But I'm afraid it brings us back to our schools again. I do interview people for jobs occasionally and I'm always very surprised to find how little the younger ones know outside their subjects. As though their whole lives had been programmed to one end only – that of getting a good job.

Mona: And could there be a better one?

Julia: Well, yes, there could. A good job is all very well, but if it's a good job that you don't like very much, then that's wasting your life. You have to find the good job. One that you can do and one that you want to do. Then you're doing something useful and being true to your self at the same time.

Janice: D'you always talk like this, Julia?

Julia: Well, yes, I'm afraid I do. Difficult to throw off the habits of a lifetime in a single afternoon.

Janice: Didn mean that. Sounds very nice.

Julia: I won't undertake to teach you to talk like that, Janice. It wouldn't help you. But if Layne would like me to teach her – well, to read and write rather better than she can do at the moment – then I would very much like to do it.

Layne: Yer. Well. Right. Thanks.

Janice: We got you all wrong. Thought you was a snotty-nosed cow.

Julia: But there is a condition, I'm afraid.
Layne: What's that then?
Julia: That you have a bath and wash your hair.
Janice: So we was right after all, Layne.
Julia: The thing is. My snotty nose has a very delicate sense of smell. And I find that the water here is always so wonderfully hot.
Patrick: Because no one else is using it, of course.
Gerald: So g-go on. G-g-give us a treat then. B-b-bimbos sh-should be a p-p-pleasure to look at.
Janice: Bimbos, you toffee-nosed twit, is kept. We ad to find our clients, not exackly every bleedin day but pretty frequent. An I've wrote it all down, Mona, like you said yesterday, an I'll read it to you. Now, if you like, in my poshest voice. It's called 'Down the Drain at King's Cross'.
Clarissa: A truly bestselling title.

Shouldn't have said that. Wonder where that word came from. Bimbo. All that effort. Thinking about words beginning with B I suppose. Done A already. Allergy, anatomy, analogy, attorney, that lot. If I go through the alphabet. A for alphabet. Got that. May find something else to remember. So. What does C stand for?

C is for Clink. O Christ. C is for Christ. Also Colombia. Most I can hope for is. Sprung and spirited away. To South America. They've got my passport. Could start again. But with Fernanda. Or Gabriella. If anyone cares at all.

C for cares. C for consideration. Getting better. But one thing is certainly certain. C for certain. You, Gerald, old son, are in dead trouble. Going to spend the rest of your life saying Si Senor to someone. Or other.

Or, of course. Destruct. Destruct.

Which begins, of course, with D.

Like despair.

Janice: I weren't quite sure where to begin, Mona. I mean my life story you said, but I can't quite remember when I was very young. Not very interestin. Nappies an that.

Clarissa: Nappies! So you come from a good home.

Layne: Yer. We juss done it. Floor. Stairs. Bed. All over.

Mona: Whatever you want us to hear, we want to hear.

Patrick: Begin at the beginning, go on to the end and then stop. Mona, there's nothing left to drink.

Mona: Well, we all get very thirsty these days. Put the empties on the trolley outside the door and ring the bell. They shouldn't be long. I don't want you to go to the kitchen at the moment, because I want you to hear this. So now, Janice. But let me say first how pleased, how more than pleased, I am that you've done it. Doesn't matter what it's like. You've done it.

Layne: Jan an I sat up alf the night. Doin mine ternight.
Janice: Right then. Are you sitting comfortable?
Julia: Impossible, I think, in this room.

V

BARRY

Janice: The first thing what I remember – I mean proper remember so's I can describe it – was me mum coming in one evening to my little room at the back. She used to lock me in while she went to work so I didn't come to no arm. An she came in with Stella. Don't really know who Stella was but she was called Stella. And me mum said: Lost me bleeding job, Stell. I'm off. And Stell said: OK. I'm bloody fed up with Brandy. Let's fuck off together. Brandy was a bloke, I should say. Er bit on the side. Not a drink. Or a dog.

Mona: Just half a second, Janice. Do you know where this was?

Janice: Well, it were in London, north side somewhere. Cos we got into a taxi an crossed the river that night and I didn't go back over again, not for some time. And it were a long time before

I was in a taxi again, I can tell you.

Julia: Can you remember the room you were locked into?

Janice: O yeh. It were a very nice little room. Had me bed and me pot. And she left me lunch on a little table. And the radio.

Julia: You would be about four, perhaps.

Janice: No, odern at. Six, I'd guess. I didn't mind. I was safe. Should've been at school ercourse but me mum never would ave nothing to do with the thorities. Snoops she called them. If ever anyone rang the bell I used to get under the bed. So did she sometimes. I used to like that. Sort of cosy. Togetherness they calls it now.

Mona: And your dad?

Janice: Never ad no dad. Told yer. Mum thought it were the postman. Got moved to another districk I expect.

Patrick: Let her get on, Mona. She has a great genius for narrative.

Janice: Yer, well, thank you, Patrick. Whatever you mean. So. We spent that night with me mum's gran. Very nice. Flowers on the wall. All in one room, me an Mum an Stell all in one big bed. But we went up the ousing next day an I remember Mum's gran saying: An take Little Wages with you. She'll put you at the ead of the queue. Always called me Little Wages. An use your proper name this time, she said. So whatever all that meant we done it. Never washed or nothin to go up the ousing. Don't want to look too posh, me mum said. So then we went to live in some really grotty flats lookin over the river with an old power station opposite.

Julia: And a very beautiful old house just in front?

Janice: Don't know about beautiful. But old. And posh. We used to tryan throw ole beer cans inter the garden but it were too far. An then they put up a sorter net. An that were when I went to school. Quite nice it was. Not far. A lotter us kids from them flats went together. Walking.

Dudley: I thought you were supposed to go in a bus.

Janice: Well probly was supposed to but we didn't never cos I don't remember that a bus ever come. If it was special. Weren't far if it weren't raining. An if it were raining we all stayed ome.

Layne: You know this place then, Julia?

Julia: Yes. There was a kind of museum in the old house.

Layne: You're weird you know that? Sit there the ole week sayin nothin an then you knows all about us.

Janice: Did you know them flats, then?

Julia: Yes. I never went into them, of course. But they should never have been built. For lots of reasons. The main one being that they were not fit for humans to live in.

Janice: Not sure if anyone ever thought we was human. Not sure if we was. An it was then at we met this man. Me an my friend Squeegee cos she was so fat. Lived next door. E ad something to do with the river cos e were only there when the tide were in. You're a nice-looking little girl e said. Ow'd you like ter do something for me? So e'd give us a shoppin bag to give an ole girl oo was sittin on a seat down by the church an she'd give us fifty pee an some sweets. Course I realise now them sweets was full of speed. An this went on some time till one day the ole girl weren't there an when we got back the bloke weren't neither. So we took the shoppin bag ome an me Mum showed it to Stell oo tasted it an said Fuckin ell I fink it's bloody eroin so we putted it down the loo. An pulled the plug. Then me mum said think we'd better scarper. So we did.

An a very good way of shovin it round I would think. Wonder ow long it went on an which ring the ole girl were in. Er mum sounds a bit like my mum. Never knows what they wants. Women ercourse. Least ats what I did think but with Mona and Clarissa an now this Julia I can't be sure of nothin. That Julia's nothin but an ole witch with er long black air an long black dress. An thin. Give er a good ug an she'd snap. Then today she wakes up sudden an starts talkin like Radio Three. Very good voice. Like that liqueur we used to have when we was in the money. Advocat. Sweet an thick. An what else does she bloody do? Offers to teach Layne to read. An done very delicate. No igh an mighty stuff. No bloody condescension. Juss came straight out an offered. Suspicious a bit. But I don't think she fancies Layne cos no one can't see what Layne looks like behind all that air.

An that poor bloody Gerald right in the shit up to is neck an over. Spooky at we should both be in ere. Someone keepin an eye on us proberly. Now oo could that be I wonder? Not that mad doctor we as to go an see very other day. If anyone's in need of is skilled services it's im imself. That fight Gerald ad with the other bloke were somethin. Ammer an tongs with broken bottles. Lads ad to break em up. Praps if I'd ad to do it I'd of got away. As it is I'm goin to stay ere as long as they'll bloody keep me. What you as to do is get on a course as lasts forever. Well a year say. Show willin that's what. Food's like shit but plenty of it an no sex ercourse. Can't even get a rise outer im at the moment neither. Nearly pulled im off this morning poor ole Pricker. But I did ave to know e were still workin OK.

That Janice is fuckin marvellous. Oughter be on the stage.

Janice: So this time it were Stell went up the ousing an I ad to be er daughter an this were a diffrent ousing from the other. Weren't so particlar as them others I mean like forms an that an so we got into a lovely tower block at the Elephant with a smashin view all over Buckinham Palace me an Stell an Mum. An it were real nice. I ad two mums, one ter take me to school an one ter bring me back. Don't know what they done in between but we was comfy. I never did learn joined-up writing but we was told about the working-class struggle an our capitalist oppressors. We ad this teacher called Two Peas cos e was always saying there's two peas in oppressors. Only thing we was on the twenty-second floor an only one lift an all the blokes comin out the pub at night used to piss in it if they wasn't bein sick. Stell used ter say them planners needs their eads examined puttin the lift there right on the street. But me mum said planners was educated people who wouldn piss in a lift if they was burstin.

Gerald: She-she was right, Janice. Educated p-people d-do it in. D-do it in their h-h-handbags.

Janice: Juss shut your face, Gerald. Blokes don't carry andbags.

Gerald: H for h-h-handbags. H-h-handcuffs. G-going t-t-too fast.

Patrick: Please continue, Janice. You have our fullest attention.

Janice: O yer. Well thank you Patrick. Them was the

good days. I went ter school reglar an we ad projects like the Peterloo Massacre an the Amritsar Massacre an the Odessa Steps an we went ter Yde Park Corner ter see the place where all them poor workin-class buggers got hanged by the neck until they was dead. But with another teacher. Two Dees this one two dees in Tolpuddle. But e wouldn never take us ter the Tower cos e said that were only fer the nobs. Ad to be proper igh class to get topped in there. So I got me mum to take me an Stell one day an the joolery were really gorgeous. Them crowns must be a bit eavy. Not what you'd want to wear at a party. An it were all very nice with Mum and Stell both in a job till one day Stell come in a bit late an said My God I've juss seen bloody Brandy. Don't think esaw me though. Well she were wrong. Three days later he were there at the front door and we never had one moment's peace from then on.

Mona: Are you reading this, Janice? It's very good.

Janice: Well not exackly reading I wouldn't say. More a kinder shorthand of my own. Notes like. Show you later. Well, I can't exactly tell what it was Stell done to Brandy cos I don't exackly know. But as soon as e got inside e welted er across the face an bloody near knocked er out. Little shitbag. Fuckin grass e said. So puttin two an two together an makin twenty-two I reckon e'd juss come out. It were about seven year since she seen im an praps it were she put im inside. Then I thought well how did Stell know that stuff we putted down the loo were heroin? Anyow what e done was tie em up seprit, took the keys an me – ostage e said – an off we went to a locksmith oo made im a complete new set. So e came to stay. Them flats was all very self-contained. We didn even know oo lived next door or opposite an I reckon they was sound-proofed too cos we never eard anything from them. Well I slides over the next few years cos I can't bear to remember an goes on to the time when –

Mona: No, no, Janice. You must tell us. You must get it out of your system. It's old memories like that that do the damage, creeping into corners and going sour. I think you said earlier that your mother married?

Janice: Yer, she did. She married bloody Brandy. An that's somethin else I don't unnerstand, why she done it. It came out Stell ad a bloke somewhere called Clive an they was actually married. So Brandy said e didn want no bigamy charge – though it would of been Stell's problem – an married my mum instead. Don't know why she done it. Though you'd ave ter be pretty bloody

> brave when the old geezer asks if you take this bloke an all that ter say No I fuckin don't. E were a great one fer tyin people up an e left Stell an me tied up in different rooms while e went off ter the Register with me mum. An when he come back e says ter me you can call me bloody dad now an ternight we'll ave a nice bitter consummation with my wife, my bitter stuff an me daughter. An e did too. Makes me sick to remember.

S&M talk like this brings Pricker right up usual. E's not well. I can tell. Limp. Not interested. What that geezer upstairs calls a side effeck I reckon. Janice is a bit dirty lookin but Pricker likes em dirty. Layne is juss bloody filthy but Pricker don't mind that. An Clarissa e would fancy clean or dirty. Can't make im out. Course what e really likes is a bloody good punch-up with blokes. You can bash blokes longern birds. Coupla good welts an birds collapses. Blokes you can go on punching em in the ribs a long time. E used to like that. E'd come up when someone tried ter bash me. Specially when I started in on the bashin meself. E'd get really excited then. Roughin up birds don't turn me on. Not like this Brandy. Ad to tie em up too. Always came to me willin. Nearly always. Best time was when I were with the Big Gaffer and there was this bloke in the cellar. Tied by is wrists to an ook. Now Barry e says we don't want no marks but I wants to ear is ribs crack. Till e talks. So I uses im like a punchball an e creaked an groaned an finally e cracks an tells the Gaffer whatever it were e wanted ter know. Then e says ter me you can finish im off now so I its im a real good crack under the chin an comes off at the same time. Never forget that. Never done it since. Fuckin gorgeous. Wonder where the Big Gaffer is now. Wouldn surprise me to find e owned this place.

That Janice lookin a bit green. Wonder what that Brandy's gettin up to.

Dudley: But he must have spent a fortune on French letters or whatever you call them now.

Janice: Only ever used one. At a time that is. Reckon e bloody washed it every day. Came in with it dangling. Bollock naked ercourse. E'd ad two eyes tattooed on is tits with is nipples bein the black bits so e was lookin at you always. An a big erection tattooed right up to is belly button an a snake curled round is actual. An Christ was e eavy. Once e were there on top you couldn ardly breathe let alone move.

Julia: I think I'm going to be sick.

Mona: O dear. Again?

Clarissa: What do you mean – again?

Mona: Julia left her lunch on the hall floor but I expect it's been cleared up now.

Clarissa: I'll come with you if you like.

Julia: Yes. Thank you. That would be kind.

Mona: Don't feel you have to go on, Janice. We're all beginning to understand. And there's lots of time.

Patrick: What d'you think Brandy had on your mum and Stella? Was he blackmailing them?

Janice: Must of been. Kind of anyow. E knew all the dodges, fiddlin the meters, gettin new child benefit book an that. E always ad money but e didn't sign on. Least I don't think e did cos e always went out Tuesdays not Thursdays. An when e went out one of us were handcuffed to the pipes either in the kitchen or the bathroom. They was on two floors. Maisonettes like. So we couldn't get near each other. E kept me at ome so Mum an Stell wouldn get up to no tricks. An every night I'd ear the thud thud of is big black belt on Mum or Stell an then e'd come inter me an say Open your legs little scumbag it's you what Snakey really likes.

An she's crying. Bloody Janice is bloody cryin. Quite a bloke this Brandy. Got it made. Like to meet im. Or me gaffer would. Wonder what is line were. Don't sound like drugs or e'd go out more. Lyin low praps. Or praps is ring got broke up. Could be anything. Don't suppose bloody Janice even knows. An Prickers still lyin quiet. E must be really ill. Well fuck me if bloody Darren asnt gone an sat in Clarissa's chair. Didn think e ad it in im.

Mona: Don't be silly, Darren. Clarissa's coming back.
Darren: Can sit somewhere else then. Me bum's numb.
Barry: Praps I could move im on for you, Mona?
Mona: No, no, Barry. That's the last thing we want. Clarissa won't mind sitting somewhere else.
Barry: Be most appy to oblige.
Patrick: You don't have to tell us that. Would you like my handkerchief, Janice?
Layne: Well thanks Patrick. I'll give it er.
Patrick: One thing about listening to other people's lives, it can make one's own problems seem very trivial.
Mona: Trivial if you like. But real all the same. Just because someone seems to have larger problems than you have, it doesn't mean that yours aren't large also. They're just different, that's all.
Dudley: I'm trying to imagine how Janice got away.
Layne: I'll tell you then. Jan's a bit poorly just at the mo. It were one afternoon. There were a visitor unexpected. Man. Jan don't know oo e was but e an Brandy wasn pleased ter see each other. An after a few minutes, say ten, e shouted up ter Jan ter stay in er bedroom cos e ad ter go out. Didn ave time ter tie er up like usual. An what e didn know was Jan ad a setter keys ovver own. Always ad ad from before e came. So she lets erself out an fucks off downstairs. An never went

back so she don't know what appened to er mum or Stell or Brandy. Worries er sometimes.

Mona: But didn't she get in touch with some social workers or the police? Or a home for battered wives?

Layne: Wernt a wife were she? An likes of us don't trouble trouble not till it troubles us. She ad a bitter real bad luck fyou asks me. Think she might ave got right away otherwise.

Dudley: We're all ears.

Layne: Well she juss went on walkin northlike, over Waterloo Bridge an up through Covent Garden an there when a taxi draws up sudden an a man gets out, lookin at er very close. Thought I reckernised that air, e said. Grown up bloody lovely. It were the man oo gived er the bag for the ole bag on the seat. Get in, e says. Then e says what you done with all that coke you didn give Granny Boiler? So she says I come back to look fer you but you wasn't there. No e says I wasn't. Fuzz got me. An Gran. I putted it down the toilet says Jan. Christ what a fuckin waste of beautiful stuff e says. Reckon you owes me five thousand nicker an with intrest an inflation we'll call it ten. I'm keepin you with me till you've bloody earned it. There were another bloke in the taxi oo eld er down. They shot er up. She passed out. An when she woke up she really were in

> prison. Not I mean a reglar prison but a big ouse somewhere an this time she didn get away for moran a year.

Strange ow these nobs an nobesses seems to care. Not sayin nothin. You looks at their faces an they looks – what's the word? Concerned. Right. They looks concerned. As if they fuckin cared what appened to bloody Janice. Even the fat ole girl in the tub chair seems to of woke up an be avin a listen. But ow can they care what appens to a little slag like Janice? They don't know nothin about er an she don't know nothin about them. An yet there's that friggin officer an a fashionable artist sittin there lookin like their numbers come up on the lottery an they lost the ticket.

An do we think they'd look as concerned if I started on my sob story with em? Though ter giver er due I think Janice, or Layne, were tellin the truth. Might try my sob stuff later. On the ladies. Might lap it up. Not that they're ere at the mo but I expecks they'll be back. Ow long does it take to sick up a lunch you've already sicked up? Can't tell what Mona thinks behind them giglamps. Shrewd she is in fact. Didn think much of er for starters but there's times I wonder if she doesn't know what she's talkin about.

Let's try a little run through then. Talking posh like Janice.

When I got to sixteen my mum says I'm off now Barry. You're a big boy an you can sign on an look after yourself.

I knows you don't know nothing an aven't got a skill or anythin like that but the state'll look after you like what it said. I'm going up north to marry Roy oo don't want no trouble with stepsons and oo's to blame im? I'm only thirty-three an it's not too late to start again. I said but you can't just leave me igh an dry Mum can you? O yes she says I can just watch me. An off she buggered.

So there I am without no pieces of paper cos I adn't been to ackshle school since I were twelve an I didn't know what to bloody do. Still like my mum said I were big – everywhere – specially Pricker oo when I comes to compare im were uge. So I offs up to the Meat Rack an when I comes back that night fuck me if I didn ave nearly two undred quid in me pocket. Stayed on in Mum's flat cos nobody never came to kick me out an I soon found I didn avter work every night cos there was gents around willin to pay very igh prices only to worship my Pricker. All they ever wanted to do. So I were suited.

Not sure if I can ear meself sayin all that in ere. What was that the gaffer used to say to me? You got no – something. Panash. That's right. You got no panash Barry. An I'd ave ter answer all their silly questions. The Meat Rack you ignorant ole cow is a part of Piccadilly where raunchy young studs goes to meet paunchy ole wimps. Probly no one in this room ever eard of it, not even Janice an Layne. Darren. O yes. Darren knows all about the Meat Rack.

Christ Almighty, what've we got ere? Lady Julia an Lady Clarissa comin back from bein sick together. Now

there's carin an sharin fer you. But they've put up Lady Julia's air so's you can see er face. An if she'd just put on a bitter meat reckon Pricker could fancy er too.
Sept e don't seem intrested in no one.

Mona: Do give Clarissa her chair back, Darren.
Clarissa: No, no, thank you. Not after he's been sitting on it. I'll sit on the sofa.
Mona: You look marvellous, Julia. Is it a bit better?
Julia: Yes. Thank you. I'm not sure if I can bear any more of Janice's life story today, though. And I'm sorry to be so feeble about it, Janice, because what I really do is admire you very much for the way you've come through it. If you have.
Mona: I think she's on her way through, anyway. A great landmark for her to have told us as much as she has. We know what started her off on her habit. And I think we can agree that it wasn't her fault, or rather it wasn't her wish, to start. Once on, she couldn't get off.
Clarissa: That's right, Mona. Bring us back to the straight and narrow.
Patrick: That's what we're trying to get on to after all. Or back on to. Our meetings aren't really meant to be a series of cabaret turns.
Clarissa: Well, I thought Janice was at least as good as a play and much better than most of the ones I've seen.

Dudley: Except that I don't think she was acting.
Janice: Dead right I weren't.
Mona: Is anyone else ready to tell us what started them off? Patrick, perhaps?
Patrick: Easy. Despair. Thought I'd lost my touch.
Dudley: Think I'd agree there. I was just getting older watching a country I'd loved and fought for going down the plughole. Forever as I thought. And I could do nothing about it. Drowning your sorrows it used to be called. But in the end the sorrows drowned me.
Julia: And yet you probably have a great deal to give. If you'd only admit it. Just as I have. If only I would condescend to do so.
Clarissa: Hard words, Julia. But then there have been a lot of hard words in your life.
Julia: How can you tell that?
Clarissa: You kept apologising in the loo just now. Apologising for being so much trouble, apologising for being sick, apologising for taking me out of the group. Apologising for being you in fact.
Mona: Full marks, Clarissa. A first-class assessment. Perhaps, one day, Julia will feel able to tell us why she has to apologise all the time. Because, as far as we can see, there's nothing to apologise for.
Gerald: B-b-beautiful b-brainy b-b-bird. B-b-bad at B-b-b's. B-b-b for B-barclays's. N-not that th-though. B-b-banker de something.

Janice: Why don't you paint her for us, Patrick? Not all in bright red though.

Patrick: Not at the moment, if you don't mind. A bit too L.S. Lowry. Who would have gone mad about her. But if she would just put on – shall we say – thirty pounds, then I would be very happy.

Bridget: You – you – you can have. Some of mine. Some of mine you can have. Bit over. Wait over. Wait.

Julia: Thank you, Bridget, and thank you, Patrick. A strange incentive, but I accept it.

Patrick: You have a beautiful smile.

Mona: So – does anyone else want to tell us how they started off? Barry. We haven't heard from you for a long time.

Barry: No. Well. Thinkin like. It were a bloke. Nice. What you might call educated. Met im in a pub. Offered me a smoke, dope ercourse but I didn know that. An one thing led to another.

Mona: Just to see what it was like?

Barry: Juster see what it were like.

An that's a bloody great lie too but what can I say ter this lot? Not without panash I can't. It were that fuckin Theo short for Theodore but don't you ever use it. When e found out Pricker didn really go for blokes we tried bloody everything. E ad the lot. Rollin. Nice pad near South Ken. So we snorted an smoked an smacked an shot up till one day e come in in a bird's frock an a turban. Looked like that grotty ole slag in Coronation Street. An I welted im. Punched im up proper. O do it again e kepp sayin don't never stop an Pricker came up beautiful so we really knew where we was. Im stuck on S&M an me stuck on smack.

Bit awkward as you might say.

Saw im reggelar. Big session every week. Till I got a bug an missed out twice. So when I got back on course I found a crowd outsider is house an a copper onner door. Bloke in the crowd told me e'd been found battered to death as they say in the papers wearin a woman's dressing gown. So I scarpered. Like me mum. Shit scared. But it weren't me. Sure erthat. Some things I done on igh which I can't remember but I never done that. Why would I want to at undred quidder time? May be a bit daft but not bloody barmy.

Long time since I thought about im. That Mona. Spose ats what she's sposed ter be doin, gettin us ter remember. An spout it all out. Buggered if I'll do that. Went back onner Meat Rack. Bitter luck the Gaffer findin me there. Don't want blokes oo makes trouble e says. Least not trouble fer me. But I likes em to make trouble for others so you come with me an we'll cause a bitter avoc in a pub just around ere. So we goes in an e tells me ter ask for five undred an sixty eight millilitres of beer. Done it afore e says. Very effective. Wot you mean sezzer barman so I repeats it an e goes on sayin e don't know what I means an then the gaffer come along an says in a posh voice this young man is within is rights you give im five undred an sixty eight millilitres er beer or I'll complain ter the perlice. You means a pint I spose sezzer barman an e gives me a pint. So er gaffer asks fra empty glass an e takes one er them tiny little medsin spoons outer is pocket an starts measurin an fuck me if it aint short. Twenny little medsin spoons. All in dead silence. Well talk about a bloody riot. That place were wrecked almost afore we got outer it. You'll do e says you'll do perfick an that were a beginnin of my new life.

Wonder where e is.

I'm ere.

An bloody Prickers moran alf dead.

Bridget: No, no, it was all. A sub. A subscription from the doctor.

Dudley: And some time ago perhaps.

Bridget: Yes a long time. Made it possible. My husband. Married life. My. It made my married life possible.

Patrick: Fantastic advertisement for matrimony.

Julia: I can't quite remember the statistics. But if one person in four marries the wrong person, then only half the population is happily married.

Patrick: Janice is the one who's going to join Mensa.

Mona: And what did the doctor give you, Bridget?

Bridget: O my lovely. My lovely lily-of-the-vallium. There. I said that. And I'm talking. Paking tart.

Mona: Yes, indeed. And we're all delighted that you are.

Bridget: Not asleep. All the time. I have been not asleep all the time. Listening.

Dudley: And very fascinating listening it is, too. A new world. To an old codger like me.

Janice: Wouldn say codger, Uncle. Fogey more like.

Layne: Nar, Jan, fogeys is weird. Remember at one we used ter call the Luton Turnoff?

Janice: Couldn forget im. The bogey fogey.

Clarissa: Tell us about him, then. That is, if you think we can stand it.

Janice: Well e were very unusual. I mean, not like nobody else. Rolled up one afternoon, putter undred quid on the sideboard an said e oped we ad a baby's bottle.

Layne: Which as it appened we adnt. Everythin else juster bout but not that.

Janice: But it weren't difficult to find one. Then it ad to be filled with milk. Blood eat exackly. Then Layne ad ter stuff it up er – what did e call it, Layne?

Layne: Me orifice.

Janice: Right. Up er orifice an then e drank the milk outer the bottle.

Layne: An come off all over the floor. We thought e was dead the first time.

Barry: An e gave yer undred nicker fer that?

Janice: Yer. Came once a week regular.

Barry: Been underpricing meself.

Clarissa: So – rent boy and hit man. Very original.

Layne: Two of us remember.

Barry: So what did Janice do turn er money?

Layne: Ad ter sing didn she? Rock a bye baby on the treetop.

Janice: It were quite OK if you didn look. Course you couldn keep yer eyes shut the ole time. Came from Milton Keynes really.

Layne: Uncle's not a bit like im, Jan. Not a fogey.

Dudley: And very relieved I am.

Janice: More like what we used ter call a DOG. Distinguished Old Gentleman. But we never got mennier them.

VI

JANICE

Patrick: This fascinating underworld life that you and Layne seem to have shared – where was it? and when?

Layne: Juss now. Three weeks praps.

Janice: Down a drain in King's Cross. Told yer. But I don't wanter upset Julia no more. She's gone green again.

Mona: She's having to get used to food again.

Barry: Ave ter be bloody strong ter get used ter this food.

Dudley: Easy to tell you've never been in the Army.

Barry: Army's fer mugs. Spends all yer life takin orders.

Mona: Perhaps this would be a good moment, Barry, to tell us about your very constructive morning. In your best English, please.

Barry: O. Yer. Well.

Mona: Some of us are having just a little difficulty understanding you.

Barry: OK. Well. I started one of them courses you was on about last week.

Janice: Blimey. Which one?

Barry: The Course Mother is entitled Mrs Pryce-Whetstone.

Mona: Flower arranging? Barry, that's for the girls.

Barry: Sexist, Mona. Sexist. Just you watch your blooming words.

Janice: Right, Mona. Me an Layne's goin on the weight-lifters course tomorrer. Just watch us.

Mona: I'm rather afraid –

Janice: There isn't one? Well, Barry'll tell us what to do. You only as to supply the dumbells.

Gerald: D-d-d for d-dumbells. D-dumb blondes.

Clarissa: Well, go on, Barry. We're all dying to know how to arrange a flower.

Barry: Yer. Well. Mrs Pryce-Whetstone says I gotta lotta talent.

Julia: But not, perhaps, for flower arranging?

Barry: Thing was, being a governmen course and that –

Mona: It is not a government course.

Barry: There were rather a shortage of material. Like waiting for the subsidy to come through like. So we just ad these stones, some big stones, some little stones, some middling stones, some big green leaves what she called artichoke leaves, six dahlias an a crysanth. I knowed it were a crysanth cos I'd seen crysanths afore but the dahlias was new. An the leaves. So what we ad to do were this. She gave us all a flat dish an this stuff. Wasis she called it. An you put some water in the dish with the stuff. Then you id the stuff with the stones. An then you stuck the leaves an flowers into the stuff through the cracks in the stones. Nothin to it.

Patrick: But tell us more. Exactly what you did.

Barry: Well, we was allowed to cut the stalks off them dahlias if we wanted. So I started at the bottom with the little stones, made a sorter mountain with the biggest one on the top. Then I puts the six dahlias, eads only, inter the stones. Zif they was climbing the mountain you might say. Then a bit igher up the crysanth. Then the leaves comin outer the top like a – like a – she did tell me what but I've forgot the word.

Clarissa: Not volcano by any chance?

Barry: Right on. Volcano. But Mrs Pryce-Whetstone said she wanted a more nusual title for er exhibition. So oner them really weird girls from oner them other groups were next to me. Makin a right mess of er dahlias. She said couldn bear ter cutemoff in their prime. Ad a kinder bandage er red see-through stuff round er eyes so I said to er what's that for an she said I still got track marks at the ends of me eyes an I said Go on an she took the bandage off an bugger me she ad.

Layne: I got summer them. An between my fingers so's no one can't see em.

Mona: But you've stopped picking at your hands. I had noticed. It's a very good sign. But go on, Barry.

Barry: Well this girl said as she'd elp me find a title an after a minute she begins writin things down. Well, readin's notter zackly my thing an there was all these long words so she says ter me very polite if you as a literary problem I will inform you what I as wrote. So she ad ter teach me ter say the words and the first one were Migraine Eadache. The second were Internal Explosion. An the third was Faked Orgasm. An then she pissed off. Thin air. Well, Mrs Pryce-Whetstone weren't very keen on the third one. I spose you knows what it means, she said.

Clarissa: Bit near the bone for her. On her third husband. The Commander. Friend of my father's. There can't be two people with that name. And probably he –

Bridget: Fake. Faked. I don't see why. Why anyone bothers. To fake anything bothers.

Barry: Settled for Migraine Eadache.

Mona: What had you thought of calling it yourself?

Barry: Grave ovva Fur Coat.
Dudley: Much more appropriate.
Julia: But not quite subtle enough for Mrs Pryce-Whetstone. When is the exhibition, Barry?
Barry: As one every day she's ere. But not ere every day. But when she pick it up poor ole Eadache fall apart. Adnt stuck the stones together proper.

Sometimes I thinks I'm a bloody fool goin along with all this rubbish an sometimes I doesn't. What I'm only just gettin used to is bein treated as if I was real. A person. Oo mattered. After all that time makes you very nervous. Layne too, she says. Lucky for us we's sharin a room so's we can talk everythin over. That kinky doctor we as to see. What's e up to we asks ourselves. You've ad a very rough ride e says. You've come through an what we as to do is try an keep you this sider the curtain as you might say. But Christ it is a bloody pleasure gettin into bed every night juss me an Layne clean sheets no sex an not the sorter bloody dreams as wakes you. Not always, that is. I think praps our angel is a angel after all. Probly e's right. There's other ways of livin. Of earnin a livin.

Long time since I thought about bloody Brandy. Cor would I like to ave the angin of im. What could e ave ad on Mum an Stella? Spose you can terrorise someone inter marryin you if you juss goes on long enough. If I gets through this lot. If I gets a job. If I gets clean again. I might go an see what's appened. But oo would I bloody ask? There weren't no one in charger them flats. Ave to go down the ousin. I'd like to see that. Could you inform me my good man if my natural mother is still inabitting flat number eighty-six on the twenty-second floor? An what might be the name o your natural mother, Madam, if you would be so kind. Can't even bloody remember. If she took is.

That flat's Stell's anyway.

Course they don't call you Madam up the ousing. Or anywhere else. What's odd about this place is nobody seems ter be lookin down on us. No one callin us shitbags or scumbags. Not what Two Peas taught us that the nobs was all a lotter artless slave-drivers. An our clients now I comes to think about it wasn't exackly outer the top drawers. So praps we isn't class traitors after all comin ere an dryin out an when all's said an done learnin to behave civil. That Julia sicks up when I tells em all about bloody Brandy. God knows what she'd do if I told em about that year I spent with bloodier Raymond. Raymondo to you you pissy little whore.

So oo looks like they found their ole mother dead on the pavement when I tells em about Brandy? Darren? Barry? O no. The gents. The ole an the not so ole. An oo goes out the room? Julia an Clarissa. They cares. They juss doesn't bloody know. I says to Clarissa yesterday Well you might be a bit different if you'd been fucked rotten every night by your step-father for moran a year. O God yes, she says, I would. Is that what it's all about? You, I mean. Yes, I says. But I'm not sure. Not at all.

An our angel. What about im. E don't come from the oppressed classes. Not a downtrodden worker. A reformed monk. So e says. Couldn't face life without it altogether. So e came back to earth. Took im about a ole month ter persuade me an Layne ter come ere. What's in it for you? we kepp sayin. An e kepp sayin Never you mind what's in it for me. If I can turn you into two clean souls for God that'll be enough. All this talk about God. What you ave to do e says is go inter oner them churches, don't matter which kind, an kneel down an say Please God do something that'll make me bleeve in you.

So ere we are. Don't seem to matter what you says. Or oo to. If we could juss bleeve they didn't mean us no arm reckon it might work. Bit like bein under the bed with Mum. Used to like that.

Barry: O course the weird girl with the blindfold weren't much good at puttin the flowers inter the ackshle vase so I said as I'd do that fourer if she'd come up with another title. O course er dahlias was in a most shockin condition by now cos she'd been tryin to ram em into the wasis while they still ad long stalks so o course the stalks kepp bendin an splittin an them little stones was rollin all over the bloody floor till the ole place were like a fuckin skatin rink. So I says to er

What is we acksherly tryin ter do, do we know? An she says Yes we does we is tryin to create a work of art with the material at our disposal. Disposal I says. Fyou mean waste disposal that's where them poor ole dahlias will ave ter bloody go if you carries on ill-treatin em like that. No no she says the dahlias is the focus of the rangement you see if you can't get summer them stuck inter the wasis. Well I says I can only do that if you lets me cut them stalks down an put a point on like the crysanth. You see ow easy tis ter stick the crysanth inter the wasis. Don't never move once in its place. Don't like the colourer that crysanth she says it's brown. Never knowed there was such things as brown flowers. Been tryin ter say brown flowers the way she said it ever since but I aven't got it yet. Anyway she says why don't you give me your yellow crysanth it'll look much nicer with my dahlias than it does with yours. An I don't like my dahlias much either all them spikes. An she were right. All er dahlias ad spikes on em while mine was soft an round. Sept for some which was ard little balls an looked like they was mader plastic. An the colours. We ad twelve dahlias tween us an they was all a diffren colour so I says I don't know ow Mrs Pryce-Whetstone expecks uster produce great works of art if she don't give us proper material. Anyway we starts again though there weren't much we could do with my dahlias cos I'd cut em right down. But we made like a small rockery with wasis in two places an we stuck er long dahlias with spikes in the top an my little tiny round ones at the bottom. But we didn't ave no room for the crysanths or the artichoke leaves so we ad ter begin again with the middlin pebbles. An we didn ave much wasis leff neither so we used a lotter pebbles, the two crysanths an one artichoke. Elegant. Then Mrs Pryce-Whetstone come along an says someone ere is a genuine genius what are you going ter call it? O says this weird girl oose name is Rosanna without battin an eyelid Conception One. An that she says pointin to our previous is Conception Two. O dear says Mrs Pryce-Whetstone what a funny sense of yumour you ave an then she scarpers. Well says Rosanna I never knowed I ad a senser yumour afore I feel much better now an then bugger me if she don't pick up both er them Conceptions an smash em on the floor.

Patrick: I know just how you must have felt. We have the right to destroy ourselves, our own works of art. But not, most definitely not, someone else's.

Barry: Weren't so much the damage to civilisation by the destruction er two timeless works of floral art as the bloody mess she made all over the bloody floor. Little pebbles all over. Big pebbles. An then she starts screamin er ead off sayin I ates things with spikes. Poor dahlias I says to er they can't elp avin spikes next time you can ave the soft round ones. Then she starts yellin again this man is tryin ter rape me so Mrs Pryce-Whetsone comes along an says don't be silly Rosanna if he were tryin to rape you e'd probly succeed which were a nice compliment ercourse but not right. So then she goes off with Mrs Pryce-Whetstone an I picks up all the mess an sticks all the flowers an all the leaves inter the wasis, surrounds the lot with bloody pebbles an then the Doc comes along an says that is a very hinteresting rangment. What do you call it? O Christ I says I think this must be Conception Three. Don't be flippant e says an off e scarpers like the others. An that were the ender our class.

Bloody Barry. Barry the bruiser. Barry the paid bruiser I wouldn't wonder. Sittin there like some bloody saint or somethin lookin like e never done nothin wrong in is ole life. I bet e could tell us a tale or two. Praps if we goes on sittin ere long enough e will. E's funny though. No marks. I spose if is gaffer were peddlin ecstasy praps that's what e used. Washed down with a little acid occasional. Can cause brain damage they says. But fcourse you as to ave a brain ter damage. Wouldn be surer bout that. Got everythin else as e keeps showin us. Wouldn mind if I never saw another rampant prick again.

Just to climb into a nice clean bed every night, with something soft an sweet-smellin to cuddle. That would be eaven. Layne doesn't smell sweet yet. Still smells of fear. She were a long way down the ole when I found er. Wouldn wanter go the ole way anyway. All the dykes I knows looks like Mona. I wonder if she? Don't think so. Can't imagine nobody fancyin Mona no matter ow desprit they was. A pillhead from some shithole outside Manchester Barry called er. Very grand of Barry. Praps a London junkie is better an a pillhead from the provinces? We don't know what Mona was on yet. An I don't think she's actually power-dressed. That jacket belonged to somebody else. That's why it droops at the shoulders. Not a designer garment. Scruffy boots. Filthy skirt. It's power-dressin sort of. Bit down market, that's all.

Funny thing equality. Birds can dress up as men an nobody turns a hair. But if a bloke come into is office in a frilly cotton frock e'd probly be arrested. Lose is job anyow. We ad some pretty funny cross-dressers in our time. I think if I ever as ter do a blow-job on another Marilyn Monroe or Marlene Dietrich or Madonna I'll probly knife im. First. Funny ow they all begins with M. M for masochist. Muss tell Gerald if e ever gets to M. Now there's someone oo'll be round the bend serious in a little while. Reckon it's started already. You comes back to sanity for a little while an then bang. Off you goes. Sectioned. Nutted. As a hatter with a H. Whatever that was. Ecstasy all day an shot up forcible at night. Wonder e's still with us. If e is. Layne an I muss juss keep outer is way total.

Not that I don't think Barry's a danger as well. E's playin the good boy juss for now. A week. But I don't think it'll last very long. I would think there's a lotter things Barry don't wanter remember an if this kinder polite interrogation goes on e may find imself sayin a lotter things e don't mean ter say. Like me. Didn really mean ter tell em all about Brandy. But it's Brandy oo frightens me. Brandy I dreams about, Brandy blue an Brandy red, Brandy orange an Brandy black. That's when I wakes up an screams. Funny. You'd ave thought it'd be bloody Raymond. Fuckin pig.

Wot's it gonna be then? Drinkin our cocktail like a good girl or am I gointer give you the biggest bloody beltin you've ever ad? Got a really good one other day. Prewar fireman's. Eavy, Janice. You wouldn like your shoulders marked permanent would you? Drink up. There's a good girl.

God knows what was in them cocktails but they brought me to life all right. So's I could reelly appreciate is masculine skills e'd say. Never knew I ad so many oles before.

Patrick: No, Mona, don't say that. It's very good that Barry's been on a course. Even if it doesn't lead to anything.

Mona: But he could just as well go on a course that would lead to something.

Barry: Not off the premises I couldn't. You seem to ave forgot that.

Mona: Quite right. I had. It'll have to be education, then. What about a language?

Dudley: I should think he'd better learn his own first.

Patrick: Well, he can do that. But I have the feeling there's another problem. Reading and writing perhaps.

Mona: I don't think there's anything quite as basic as that here.

Julia: Then there should be.

Patrick: Exactly. Lots of people nowadays go to school without learning anything. It's nothing to be ashamed of. Rather the other way round.

Dudley: And just what can you mean by that?

Patrick: I mean that if you leave a state school able to read and write you should be frightfully, frightfully pleased. A real achievement against the odds.

Mona: It's not as bad as that, Patrick. You mustn't believe everything you read in the reactionary press.

Barry: E's right ferall that.

Layne: Yer. E's right. Never learned nothin tennier my schools.

Mona: But I was teaching very young children to read before – well, before I stopped teaching. How long did you stay at school, Barry?
Barry: Moved ouse when I were twelve. Ad ter register atter new school. So I never. Onter the streets instead.
Mona: But you could read by then, surely?
Barry: Nar. Never bothered. Couldn see the poin.
Mona: But you didn't have to see the point. You just had to learn to read.
Barry: Yer don't as ter know ow ter read n write ter make good money. Can write my name. An one or two other names as well. You as to when you signs on. Don't need no moran that. State supports you whatever.
Clarissa: So you signed on when you were sixteen and you've been drawing dole ever since.
Barry: Yer. Course.
Mona: But you never took a job?
Barry: Nobody never offered me one.
Dudley: Can't say I blame them altogether.
Clarissa: What can you do, Barry? Apart from the rough stuff.
Barry: Genius at rangin flowers remember? Brown flowers. You can stop gettin at me if you like. Might get cross.
Mona: O, we're not getting at you, Barry. It's just that we feel that if someone had taught you

something your life might be much easier. You might not be here for one thing.

Barry: Likes it ere acksherly. Food's bad.

Janice: Bettern you ad in your squat?

Barry: Nar. We ad good food there. There were a kebab take away an a caff. Useter sit there evenins keepin the yobs off. Free nosh. Protection.

Patrick: Performing a public service. Very commendable.

Dudley: What do you mean by that?

Gerald: F-f-fuzz had to d-do it. Otherw-wise. G-g-good work for g-g-glaziers. F f-for f-f-fuzz. G for g-glaziers. N-no f-further.

Clarissa: And that seemed to be the right thing to do?

Barry: Ercourse. We was runnin a protection racket wasn we? Owed itter are clients. All this talk bout right an wrong. If you like doin it it's right. If yer don it's wrong.

Julia: Barry, how brilliant. Disposing of all the religions, and all the philosophies, in two sentences.

Dudley: It's just this fantastic waste of public money.

Barry: Wotcher mean, waste? Oo pays taxes is the rich. Poor doesn ave to, right? Rich supports the poor OK? At's what they're for, right? Don't want no complaints about that.

Dudley: When I think of the trouble I used to have paying that damned income tax – pass me the whisky, Patrick.
Janice: Well, that's one thing e can't do, Uncle. Juss give me your paw. I'll old it while you goes through the shakes.

So ere we are then, ome an dry as you might say. Poor ole Uncle don't much like bein dry. Grippin me zif e were drownin. Shakin. Poor ole bugger. Don't never say much bout imself sept today. An that bloody Barry borin on about is responsibility to is clients in is protection racket zif e were some kinder bloody lawyer. Glad I weren't in is squat. I can imagine. Piss outer the winder an don't crap on the carpet. Sept there probly weren't no carpet. I'd like to think that's all over an done with. Difficulter know whatter think bout this setup ere. Someone muss be informin on us. Spyin. Even if Mona says it ain't a governmen project she doesn't ave ter be tellin er truth. She's alright, Mona. Bit dim. Means well. Praps it's as well I didn go on beyond bloody Brandy. Not sure oo'd really wanter know about Raymond. Not as I knows exackly but I got some very good ideas. Whoever it were I hopes e killed im very slowly. Roasted over a candle. Take about a week. Not expensive, candles. Used a lot in our time, Layne an I. Not for roastin though. Funny thing. Bout the ony thing no one never asked us to do. Can't elp thinkin I might sell my story to *Newser the World*. Sept

I don't bloody bleeve anybody'd bloody bleeve me. Ave ter write it proper too.
Dots an dashes an them things in the air.

Postrophies.

OK.

After I ad been resident – after I had been resident in my cellar – wonder how you spell that – somewhere in north London, exact location at present undisclosed for a period of time approaching that of one year approx – nearly – I were seated on my flea-ridden reposing couch awaiting the evening arrival of my lord and master fucking Raymond. I were aware – I was aware that he had been delayed beyond his normal time of appearance and I were hoping praps he wouldn't never arrive at all. When all of a sudden hoo should come in but a tall young black man hoo said his name was Orris. As the only person in possession of a key to my basement apartment – my garden flat – were bloody Raymond I greeted his arrival with surprise.

Oo the fuckin ell are you I says. Don't think I would've said hoo. Never you mind he says just pack up all your things if you got any and we will piss off from ere fastern lightning. O I says be kind enough to inform me what has occurred. Bloody Raymond got imself topped e says. O I says what joy ow too fuckin bloody marvellous let us remove from this odorous locality immediate. So we puts my non-existent possessions into a carrier bag and off we buggered out the back and over the wall. As we receded in a southerly direction it was observed that the fucking fuzz was at the front door already so we gets on to a bus which happened to be passing convenient and finished up in bloody Highgate.

So what does we do now Mister Clever I says. I know oo you is Janice he says that's ter say I don't but I know you been in there a long time an I don't erprover that. I bin tryin ter rescue you some time an now I as succeeded. Well fuck me I says you is my knight in shinin armour. Don't acksherly think the *Newser the World*'s goin ter like all these fucks. There's that lovely long word which is OK. Well penetrate me you are my knight in shining armour I observed to him in an undertone but we still hasn't got nowhere to sleep. The stars was now a-twinkling in their evening glory. Well he says actually we has but we'll go there on the tube this time.

Can't keep this up no longer. They'll ave to write it theirselves. E ad a little squat not far from King's Cross. A smashin pretty little house wither narea entrance an a little garden wither door inter a passage. No e says I don live here. You never seen me. Ere's the keys to all the doors. Make it look like you lives ere legal, put the lights on an that. Some ole girl lives ere but she's off. Got some nice furniture what was too big for me mates ter lift. I opes you'll be very appy. An e pisses off. He removed himself from my presence. An when I looked in my carrier there were another one e must of put there all stuffed with two thousand quid in ten poun notes.

Never forget that night. Long as I live. Bout two hours after my cocktail time I starts to shiver an shake an sweat an ache an creak an groan an I wanted a scream but I didn dare. Crawled inter thole girl's bed. Very comfy. Nice bedclothes too I found later. Must've been in that bed three days. Plugs pulled. Taps and water. I said to myself Janice you're free you always wanted to be free and now you are. No more cocktails. No more Raymond. No more Brandy. You have to beat this thing. So I got up and washed and went out an got some food. Went in an out by the garden door. And when I comes back in again I notices these dustbins outside the back door. Of the ouse I mean. An when I looks inside the firs one there was Layne.

Dudley: What can you be thinking about, Janice? You're clutching my hand right off.

Janice: Sorry, Uncle. I were thinking. Nothin very nice. Are you feelin better, a bit?

Clarissa: Do you want to tell us, Janice? Or is it too awful?

Janice: Well, yer, it is a bit awful. An I'm not sure of my – can't remember the word.

Patrick: Audience? Terms of reference? Confidentiality?

Janice: At's it. The last one.

Mona: Everything that's said in this room is between us. Only. Of course I understand that everyone here is very suspicious. That's the fault of the drugs. But you've got to believe that. All of you. Otherwise we shall never achieve anything.

Barry: So if I was to confess to murder you wouldn tell no one?

Julia: Difficult. Fundamental. Are we priests, psychiatrists? Or just good friends?

Janice: So tell us, Barry. Ow many villains you topped? Or was they all rozzers?

Mona: We're just good friends, in fact. But if you have murdered somebody, Barry, it would be nice if you wouldn't tell us because then we should all be accessories after the fact.

Janice: Thought accessories was something you wore. Black with shocking pink accessories.

Barry: Don't think I never done nobody in. Not direct you might say. Might've gone off later. Softened up you might say.

Julia: Dear me, Barry. Are you really a hit man? Not at all romantic, now that I come to think of it.

Clarissa: Come to Copsewood to see real life as it is actually lived. Meet the stars of the underworld.

Barry: At's enough from you. Fork-tongued bitch.

Clarissa: Fork-tongued bitch! You've been reading Shakespeare.

Barry: You knows bloody well I don't read. Not proper. At's what Rosanna called Mrs Pryce-Whetstone. Made a note. Very nice.

Mona: Making progress, making progress. Julia's started talking, Bridget sometimes, even Darren has said something. I would like to get back to our twelve steps before we forget all about them. I think we can say that we have all admitted – or have been obliged to admit – that our addictions were stronger than ourselves. The only thing to do was to overcome them. In other words, we have all taken Step One. Step Two is to consider whether a power greater than ourselves, greater even than our addiction, cannot restore us to sanity. And health.

Patrick: Depends what you mean by restore. Some of us didn't have much sanity to start with.

Clarissa: Well, that's not you, Patrick. You've got loads of sanity. And talent. You just don't condescend to use them, that's all.

Patrick: Condescend! What the hell do you mean by that?

Clarissa: Patrick, you forget that I've seen those red paintings. Anyone, any ordinary person, with that sort of ability would be painting twenty-four hours a day just for the sheer joy of being able to do it.

Patrick: Shows how much you know about the creative process. And what about the condescend, then?

VII

LAYNE

Clarissa: Hiding your light under a bushel is a sort of condescension. I'm brilliantly clever, you seem to be saying, but I'm damned if I'll prove it to the plebs.

Patrick: Or I could be saying I don't really think I'm as clever as all that but I don't want to put it to the test in case I turn out to be right.

Julia: And lose all faith in yourself?

Patrick: And lose all faith in myself. Never had much.

Mona: Then that we have to change.

Patrick: I don't see how you can do that. Since we're being so serious all of a sudden, I have to say that the greatest power in my life was the burden of my talent. Was it important? Was it there? Did it matter? Who cared? I only took to the bottle when I couldn't answer these questions. Now I can. The answer to all four is No. I've wrestled with my Satan. Not only is he behind me, he is actually underfoot. Trampled on. Dead.

Clarissa: I don't believe what I'm hearing.

Dudley: So the bottle was to fill that aching void.

Patrick: Yes.

Dudley: I know just how you felt.

Julia: And now we have to find something to replace the bottle?

Patrick: Exactly.

Clarissa: Well, I can't exactly recommend that magic mixture of smack and coke. Very expensive and it doesn't last. Wonderful while it does, though.

Mona: Not funny, Clarissa. That's all supposed to be behind you.

Clarissa: Well, it isn't. And it never will be entirely behind. What is your clever little phrase? In recovery for the rest of your life?

Gerald: W-w-what about a course. A c-c-course of M-m-mills and B-b-boon? Library's f-f-full. And other th-th-things of course. M for M-m-mills b-b-but B for B-b-boon.

Patrick: That's about as sensible as anything anyone else has said.

Julia: But perhaps there is another talent? Hidden? One that no one suspects, not even you?

Patrick: No one ever thought I had any talent at all.

Clarissa: But Patrick, does it never occur to you that all those other people could be wrong?

black. everythin in me eads black. empty. like that thing uncle said. achin void. then sometimes theres a crack in the black. a chink. but im still afraid of whats goin ter come through it. an no noise in me ead. everyfings silent. i spose if its dead its silent. me eads dead. probly im dead too. wouldn mind really. bein alive werent exackly a lot of fun. in fack its been what clarissa calls sheer ell. cant elp likin clarissa. shed ave stood up ter them bastards in them omes. dont ardly like to think what theyd ave done to er if she ad. im not never goin ter say their bloody names again. an why does the soun of runnin water still make me feel sick. we as baths ere. i dont. but ere is alright. glad i came now. in fack i wakes up in the morning an wonders where i is an when i remembers i feels really appy. sept for the black in me ead. wish itd go. praps there wouldn be nothin else if it did go. dont see ow thatterd matter. nothin is nothin. no difference tween one sorter nothin an another.

course as jan keeps tellin me its not cos i cant remember its because i dont wanter remember. an i dont wanter remember. i dont wanter remember somethin i cant remember. screw loose there. always did say there were somethin missin. them. not me. them. never thought there were nothin wrong with me. juss nobody never tried to fine out what i could do. i dont know nothin cos nobody never taught me nothin but it dont mean i cant learn if i gets a teacher. well jans teachin me. says im very quick. nobody never said that afore cos nobody never tried to fine out. but i lissens ter all this igh talk an i dont unnerstan moran arfer it. but the arf i does unnerstan i likes very much. so praps im ony arf crasy. wich would be an improvemen.

an i feels safe ere. dont remember i ever felt safe afore. sept with jan in our squat. but even then we never knowed what were comin in through that door. not to start with you didnt. then they come back. gain an again. so then you did know. what they wanted. what you adter do. an the bloody money they all anded over. where did they bloody get it? still they gave it us sos we could stay where we was. sos they could come again. cosy. i can remember feelins all right. that one anyow. but its still black. nothin on the screen like. power cut. do not reajuss your set. well this set does need a reajuss. praps thats why im ere. bein serviced.

o ell. o bloody fuckin ell. that shittin rubbishin word. why did i ever use it? why did it come through the door? im goin ter service you you rotten little scumbag like you never been serviced afore. me an my fren sir. an youll call us sir wile we does it an youll like it an youll say thank you an youll keep your fuckin bloody little mouth shut or well slap you so ard you wont never get up again. ever. its that voice. i can ear it. i can feel what i felt. but i cant see. still black. but i dont wanter see. dont want that door open. someone might come in.

Janice: Isn't that right, Layne?
Layne: Isn't what right?

Janice: O dear. You been dreamin again? Told you not to. You never knows what's goin ter come back. Clarissa says other people's very often wrong. That praps we shouldn accep their opinion all the time. An I says they can make big mistakes which you can't do nothin about cos you asnt any power. An that really is a power greater than us. So I says Layne knows all about that.

Layne: Yer. The thorities. Once you gets inter their power you never gets out again. Social workers. Sollogists. Collogists. Magistrits. Kermittys. Then they bungs you away in some ome an forgets all about you.

Julia: Tell us about it, Layne. If you can.

Layne: Notter day. Said too much.

Julia: Would you mind if Janice tells us? If she knows.

Layne: O she knows alright. You tell em, Jan.

Janice: Right then. It were our angel oo explained all this though Christ knows ow e foun out. But in the Midlands somewhere there's two omes one called Langton an one called Langham.

Mona: Yes, that's right. One for disturbed and one for delinquent children.

Janice: Well, there were a cock-up. Computer got confused. Layne were senter the one for delinquents when she were really disturbed.

Dudley: Damn disgraceful if that's true. How could anyone be so careless? When I think of the salaries they're all getting it's perfectly monstrous. More than monstrous. Outrageous. Actionable. Is Layne doing anything about it?

Janice: Not Layne erself exackly but I think our angel's still snoopin about. Says e can't do nothing till Layne remembers it all erself.

Julia: How did you meet Layne, Janice? It seems to have been very lucky for her.

Janice: O dear. Shall I tell em, Layne?

Layne: Yer, tell em. Then we's all sessories. Equal.

Janice: Right then. I can tell you where I foun er but what we still doesn know is ow she got there. Bits of er memry is juss blank. So. I were in a squat on me own. Very classy, small ouse near King's Cross. Don't ave ter tell yer ow I got there. But I went through ell all by myself for a few days when I got there an then I thought I better get some food so I wennout an when I come back there was these dustbins. An I opened the firs one an there were Layne.

Patrick: You just have to be joking.

Clarissa: But can one really get into a dustbin and put the lid on afterwards?

Janice: Don't know about that. Reckon someone else put the lid on. But it were a big new one. Green. Plastic. Anyow I thought she were dead when I saw er first an I am ashamed ter say my firs thought were O ell now I'll ave ter leave this very comfortable squat. But when I touched er she were warm.

Julia: Brave.

Janice: Well I weren't very strong juss at that time not avin been very well fed lately an I couldn lift er. Thought she were asleep. So I lays the dustbin down gentle an pulls er out. She were a really grisly sight sick all over er track marks everywhere you could think of an in a lotter places you couldn think of. She were thin all skin an bone an she were wearin a black plastic dustbin liner. Upside down like. So I juss as ter letter lie on the ground till she come to. Cleaned er up a bit. An waited. She were stoned right out an I were afraid she'd snuff it cos then I'd be in the shit too. But she didn. She were breathin alright an she juss lay there. Lucky it were summer. Lay there eight hours. Reckon they was the longest eight hours of my ole life.

Dudley: I'll bet they were. You're a heroine, Janice. Would you like to hold my hand this time?

Janice: Kind of you, Uncle. But I don't think Layne'd let me go.

Clarissa: So – tell us more. Very romantic in a way.

Janice: Not at the time it weren't. When she woke up she starts screamin an cryin but I couldn unnerstan a word she said. Thought she were foreign. Then she comes to sort of an I gets er to bed. Washes er a bit more an she passes out again. Well I thought I gotter get some food downner or she'll starve ter death but she couldn take nothin but water. An she kepp sayin Don touch me I'm dirty I'm dirty I'll never get clean again. Well ercourse turned out she ad a very expensive abit. When she come to proper she tells me where ter go an what ter get an as I ad a bitter money juss then I did. The bloke I went to put us inner way of earnin what we need ter feed Layne's abit an we lived like that moran a year.

Mona: But you could have got help. Drug addiction centres, even a doctor would have helped you.

Janice: Mona, you juss eard Layne say about the thorities. She wouldn ave gone. Not sure I would either. With the thorities you never knows oose side they're on an the risk's juss too big ter take. They should all ave a big notice sayin We is not the perlice everythin confidential.

Mona: Many of them do. More or less.

Janice: O. Well. You ave ter go there ter fine out, don't you? An if the notice aint there it's a bit late.

janice is a purl of great price. i do not know what i would of done if janice ad not of foun me in that dustbin. born in a squat. growed up in a dustbin. wot a life. cant be true though. no one grows up in a dustbin. black still. blank. ats a new word. blank. cant think of anythin ter think of. when im on igh i remembers a lot of things but i forgets em again when im on low. an i been on low ever since i got ere. dont mind bein on low. restful. ats what jan calls me. restful. id like ter be restful rester my life.

funny ow i remembers them geezers oo use ter come in. not always at night either. them an their weird ideas. we ad quite a wardrobe by the end. all them feathers an leather belts. brought their own stuff usual. we juss ad ter know wich one were next. jan did that. make a good seckiterry angel says. but i knows e really wants er ter be prime minister. but wot was odd about them geezers was they never wanted – contack we called it. we touch them but they never touch us. well said jan suits me ive ad enough contack ter last me the rester my life. you too she says even if you cant remember. but ill remember one day she says. be nice ter remember today. OK. i will think about all them things as i cant remember. then praps itll all come back.

well i remembers pindown alright. a little room all cream an grey with igh locks on the winders an a door you couldn get out of. an you made your bed an cleaned the room an that were about it. meals come in. the sirs come in an talked like they was vestigatin a murder an all i ever said was i never done nothin i never done nothin in me ole life an that were quite true. but all that were before. before the thing. an i cant remember wot appened atween them an the dustbin. not when im on low i cant. theyll ave ter give me another fix or i wont never remember nothin. but i promise jan i wont never ave another fix.

so i wont.

its not far off. now i got that voice talkin to me. i remembers at voice. ill always remember at voice. wish i didn. wish i didn ave to. mona says ill feel better when i tell em but wot ave i got ter tell em? course nobody dont know that. not even me.

Clarissa: So how did your idyllic existence in this charming little house come to an end?
Janice: Well, the ole girl come back, didn't she?
Barry: Bet she adder stroke onner front door step.
Janice: Not er. She were a really splendid ole girl. We change the locks. All on em. So she ad ter ring the bell to get into er own house. And oo are you may I ask she says I am the tenant of this ouse I says. O no you are not she says. This ouse as not been let for over a year I am the owner of this ouse. Well o course I ad acksherly guessed that so I says Well Madam we is acksherly care-takin on your behalf. This ouse were extensively burgled afore we come inter it there is only the eavy furniture left. Which might be better in a museum safer anyow. But we as kepp it clean an done a bitter paintin and the burglars aint never come back. So she says I suppose you think I owe you a debt of gratitude an I says in a manner of speaking yes this ere is no locality for the likes of you. My grandfather built this house she says an I am very fond of it. Yes I says it is a very nice ouse we as been very appy.

Julia: But what about your – premises?
Janice: Well, they was in the basement of course. Never used the ouse proper. We lived up there an kept it nice. But she went down before very long and when she come up she says – an I won't never forget this – you appear to be carrying on some kind of business in the basement. Yes, I says, you could call it that. Well, she says, you will cease trading from this moment. Cease trading. What beautiful words. Is the telephone in order she says. Don't know I says we never tried. I appears to ave been mistaken in you. The bank is supposed to pay the telephone. Perhaps it did. But it were working an she says to this person Bernard I as two problems for you – cos she'd seen Layne snorin er ead off upstairs – come over at once. An it were our angel.
Patrick: Almost, almost, enough to restore one's faith in human nature.
Clarissa: Did you ever have any?
Patrick: Well, do you know, I think I did. When I was very young. About your age, Clarissa.
Gerald: C-c-curious. F-f-flames never s-s-seem to g-g-get the s-s-snakes. T-t-tongue eats them b-b-but they c-c-come b-b-back. B-B-B for B-b-bird. B-B-B for Barcelona. B-B-Barcelona. N-not th-that. B-B-Banco.
Clarissa: Mona, shouldn't you do something about him? The doctor perhaps?

Mona: I don't like to disturb him at this time of the afternoon. Just don't pay any attention.
Patrick: I'll get him some water to put out the flames. Dying of thirst myself anyway.
Gerald: B-b-bring a h-h-hosepipe. M-m-m-mongoose f-f-for the s-s-snakes.
Patrick: Doubt of their being available quite immediately, old man. But surely, Mona, the tea must be there by now?
Mona: Yes, it should be. Just bring it in. I don't want to break us up yet.
Clarissa: No. Getting quite interesting. At last.
Mona: There should be a trolley in the hall. I begin to feel that Layne may have something to tell us quite soon.
Gerald: T-t-tea won't do. B-b-bring a h-h-hose. H-hose me down. Or l-l-let me g-g-go and have a sh-sh-shower. Sh-sh-shivering.
Layne: No, no. No. No. A shower. A shower. A shower. Go an wait in the shower little scumbag. Old me and, Jan. I can't say it. I'll go mad if I remember.
Mona: Just hold her hand, Janice. And don't press her. We'll talk about something else while we have tea.

i dont want to tell em. im not a dog. dogs is well treated. no one never treated me well not afore jan. but i remembers now. that voice. wait in the shower little scumbag. always late at night. always dark. silent. sept that voice. wisperin almost. do as i say or ill welt yer. keep yer bloody little mouth shut or ill welt yer. no onell notice. on pindown aint yer? wots a few bruises in there?

i cant go on more. but theres light there now. not the ole screen aint blank. i been reajussted. long word. where do i remember it from? we never ad no telly on pindown. right. right. draw the curtain. there were a curtain. a curtain to the shower. and one of em inside it. inside it. waitin. juss waitin fer me.

Layne: I can't, Jan. I can't tell anyone. Not even you.
Janice: You can, Layne. You'll never be right till you tells us. Let me elp you then. There was these two blokes. You calls them Sirs but they sounds more like night nurses or night watchmen or somethin like that. An one er them would wake you up an tell you ter go to the shower room. Where the other was waitin. An you was wearin – what was you wearin, Layne?
Layne: Juss me shift. Me nightie. Never ad no buttons on pindown.
Janice: So the one in the shower were there starkers, right? E'd take off your shift while the other stripped isself, right? Then e'd turn on the shower an you'd all get in an they'd use a lotter soap.
Layne: I can't say it, Jan.

Janice: Juss say it. Say it for me, Layne. You never as. We never got as far as the shower room afore. Spit it out. Let em all ear. They all loves you, Layne. They'll be angry for you. Not with you. But you gotter tell em.

Layne: Don't want em angry.

Janice: Angry for you, not at you. What did they do?

Layne: Got up me. One up the front an one up the back.

Janice: Well done, well done. Lovely. Just say it again. Go on.

Layne: One up the front an one up the back.

Janice: An it weren't your fault. You couldn elp it.

Layne: It weren't my fault. I couldn elp it. They were so bloody strong.

Bridget: No, no. No, no. You must tell us. You must tell. They must be pross. Prostate. They must be persecuted. You will be. It will poison. Poison your whole life.

VIII

DUDLEY

Mona: I wish we could arrange that. But I don't think Layne knows who they were.

Janice: Always the same two. Praps once a week. But at night. Not sure she could reckernise them.

Bridget: You mustn't let them. Not let them get. Get away with it. The most awful thing. It is the most awful fling. To a girl that can happen. How was she then? Old.

Janice: She don't know. She runned away when she got outer pindown. Gotter way ter London. But then she can't remember nothin till I finds er in the dustbin. Not even when she's igh.

Mona: Here is Patrick with the tea. We are all very pleased to see you.

Dudley: Don't remember ever being so glad to see a cup of tea.

Clarissa: Sit still, Uncle. I'll bring it to you, like a gentleman.

A gentleman. I wonder if my poxy little grandson had any idea of what he was pitchforking me into. You tarnish my image, Granpa. I'm having you dried out. Like being put in some kind of oven. And what is his image, his precious image? He is a whizz-kid advertising exec who specialises in multipurpose telly ads, the ones that you don't know what they're for. He did that really disgusting one for beer all by himself. You'd think an advertiser noted for his alcohol ads might be rather enhanced by a drunken old soak of a grandfather. But no. You tarnish my image, Granpa. Just as if I were his grandson.

And in my day if something was extensively advertised you knew there was something wrong with it. But not now. They've just devalued every word in the English language and unsettled half the nation.

He pays more for one of those suits that don't fit than you have to pay for one that does. So how idiotic can you get? Not what I fought for. Not what I fought for at all. I get a strange picture of his generation here. He's twenty-six. So we have Barry the bruiser, illiterate, immoral, completely unaware when he's breaking the law. Gerald's a bit older and he can probably read. But look at the trouble he's in already. Those two maniacs who took Layne into the shower are about the same age I expect. Janice is the stuff heroes are made of. Not her fault her schooling was, well, interrupted. Layne I can't bear to think about. And as for that little black boy on the chair beside me he seems to have been run over by a steam roller. Not that sort of black. I do not mean, my dear Madam, that he is of African descent. He has black hair, nearly black eyes and a pale pink skin generously decorated with purple pimples. Not what you might call a superb specimen of Caucasian manhood but presumably educated by the public exchequer. Thank God I shall be dead long before they take over the country.

Clarissa: Here you are, Uncle. Milk but no sugar.
Dudley: Thank you, Clarissa. Very kind. Perhaps Darren would like some tea? Why don't you go and get some?
Darren: Cos I don't want no tea an Clarissa will whip my place if I leaves it empty.
Clarissa: Spoken like a true Brit, Darren. But I'll get you some tea if you want some.
Darren: Tea is for poofs.
Clarissa: Well thank you, Darren. I'm sure Barry will be very surprised to hear that.
Dudley: I daresay the one who really needs some tea is Layne. If you think she's finished crying.
Clarissa: I'll go and see.

That poor old girl stuck in the chair. What made her suddenly come to life, I wonder? Who raped her in a shower? Not an old girl at all really. Must be ten years younger than I am. Would be pretty if she wasn't so fat. Simmer very slowly in cream and serve with red currant jelly. Madame Michelin. She and Darren are the only two who really haven't said anything. Julia doesn't say much but today she has come out as a person. Rather a good person. Can't think of the old girl's name. I mustn't call her that. She's not as old as I am, not by any means. I really hate that old man in the mirror. Bridget, that's what she's called.

I would place her on the 'Yes, dear' circuit. Thought that model had been discontinued years ago. Strange the way the women have taken over the world since they started wearing boots. That you could see, I mean. End of the sixties I should say. Don't think the mess the world's in is entirely their fault but they've made a handsome contribution. Making difficulties unnecessarily. Of course what's really wrong is that the NCOs have disappeared. Some became officers and some joined the men. A few of my *havildars* would soon put them right. But no more Gurkhas. Disbanded. All have to go back to Nepal and work on the land. Nothing else to do and they'll hate that. Some people thrive as fighters. For just causes of course. That's where the arguments come in. Some causes are juster than others.

But just think of an army made up of people like Gerald. Barry you could train if you had enough time. About ten years to teach him the difference between his right and his left. But Gerald. What would he do if he were to be stranded in the desert? Sit down and yell for Mummy to bring him his bucket and spade. They forgot about initiative, whoever brought them up. You don't have to be able to spell it, but you do have to know what it is. And shame. They seem to have no sense of shame. Probably we had too much. Inhibited us. But they seem to have none at all. A quick fuck means about as much as a quick shit. A nation of wimps and pimps.

Clarissa: I'll take your cup, Uncle. I think Mona wants to get started again.
Dudley: Yes. Thank you. I'm sorry you can't come and sit here.
Clarissa: I'm quite OK on the sofa.
Mona: Is Gerald better now, Patrick? Are the fires out?
Gerald: N-n-not out b-b-but b-b-better. The s-snakes are s-s-still b-b-bad.
Julia: Take a few deep breaths, Gerald. It sometimes helps.
Gerald: My l-l-legs are f-f-falling off.
Mona: Well, they aren't really. If you sit quietly they'll come back again. And Layne? How is she?
Janice: All right, I think. Probly won't talk no more.
Mona: It would be so much better for her if she would.
Julia: That was wonderful of you, Janice. To get her to tell us what was really worrying her.

Janice: Juss feels dirty all the time, she says.
Bridget: But she mustn't. Not feel dirty. Not her fault. Those men. Without her conn. Content. They did it against her. Against her. No need to feel filthy. Guilty. Her will.
Layne: Still do though. Think they thought I liked it. Privlege ter be done by two blokes at once. Always ad ter say thank you. On my knees.
Dudley: Monstrous. Outrageous. No words. Speechless.
Julia: It seems a silly thing to say, but you must try to forget. You've shared it with us. You've survived. And if you will let me I could help to build up the new you. I'd like that.
Janice: Think Layne would, too. Could try at least.
Bridget: But those men. Other girls. How is she? How old is she?
Mona: The doctor thinks she must now be seventeen. But it's difficult to tell because she is still seriously under-nourished. Not because Janice didn't feed her properly but because her – habit – prevented the food from doing her any good.
Patrick: Then they had better get another cook. That lunch today was especially revolting. If Julia and Layne have to be persuaded to eat, then the food has to be worth eating.
Julia: Thank you, Patrick. My thoughts exactly.
Dudley: Get up a petition.

Mona: Well, why not. And try and find those men.
Layne: I'd reckernise that voice. Anywhere.
Gerald: M-m-my right f-f-foot's f-f-fallen off.
Mona: Perhaps Barry would put it back on again.
Barry: Yer. Well. Why not. This one, is it? Does it clip on – or does you ave ter screw it?
Gerald: P-p-push it back on. T-t-tighten th-th-the other one. B-b-better. Th-th-thanks.
Barry: Should be OK now. Keep em still if I was you.

I know how Gerald feels. It wasn't snakes and flames. It was bats and mice and seagulls bombing. And sometimes I would scream so loud that I would wake myself. No one to hear of course. Upstairs perhaps. If they heard I expect they just thought it was that old wino going bonkers again. Which it was of course. I covered all the mirrors except the one in the hall. It was too big. So I covered me every time I went past it. Or crawled. Think I crawled most of the time. Not so far to fall if you're on the floor already. And if I do dry out. If I do get rid of what Mona calls my habit I expect. What then?

She is still the most beautiful girl I have ever seen. Why did she have to go and die? Olivia. Olivia Holden. One Indian great-grandmother which she kept a great secret. Elegant. Kind. Resourceful. Loving. Everything one could possibly want. Haflong was a charming little place. A railway town miles from anywhere. Club. Golf course. Tennis. The usual things. Just much more beautiful than most places. Bit hilly for someone nursing a gammy leg. Not gammy any more. And then thirty wonderful years. Rupert. We really worshipped that boy. Both of us. Singapore. Borneo. Hong Kong. Wherever we went he came, laughing, cheerful, never phased. Kuala Lumpur. Penang. Then here. I suppose his education was a bit haphazard. But to marry that frightful young woman from Weybridge in his first year at Sussex. I have to belong somewhere, Pop, he said. Yes, I said, but it doesn't have to be Weybridge. That's where Sheila is, he said. And that's where they went.

I would no more admit to having a grandson called Clifford than he would to having a drunken old granpa. So what is it? Meals on Wheels. District Nurses. Killed with kindness. Can never decide if they think I'm a cat or a dog or a budgie. Alcoholics Anonymous. The DHSS. No H any more. Regimental reunions when I can afford it. Telly. Bowls. A grey vista of meaningless boredom. Breast cancer. Why didn't she tell someone? And Rupert. A motorway pile-up. Not his fault. Somewhere in the middle. Sometimes I think I would prefer the mice and the seagulls. And the bats. And the flying foxes. Sometimes the seagulls turned into flying foxes. And they all had teeth. I wonder if Gerald's have teeth. Snakes don't, I suppose. Or flames. And the thought that they might want me to go and live with them – just to keep an eye on you, Granpa.

Not Weybridge any more.

Hartley Wintney.

O my God.

Mona: Did you say something, Dudley?
Dudley: Don't think so. Just groaned.
Clarissa: Groaning is not allowed, Uncle. It's sweetness and light day all of a sudden. We are discussing Purpose; but you were a long way away.
Janice: Where was you, Uncle? You looked so happy for a moment.
Dudley: I was in India. Falling in love with my wife.
Mona: Do you want to tell us?
Dudley: Not particularly. It's a very private, very perfect part of my life and the only person I really shared it with has gone.
Patrick: Leaving an unbearable gap.
Dudley: As you say, Patrick. But it's a gap that can never be filled because it was left by a person, and I don't think I shall ever meet another person quite like her. Very often in India it would say on the label 'This is a genuine article. Beware of substitutes'. And then you knew it had been made in Japan and was as ungenuine as possible. But I still tend to beware of substitutes.
Julia: I don't think replacements are necessarily substitutes. Nothing is quite like anything else. A thing can comfortably take the place of another thing so long as it is not expected to be exactly like that thing.
Clarissa: So you can replace a horse with a cow?

Julia: Yes, as long as you don't expect the cow to behave like a horse. A completely different kind of relationship but it could be just as fulfilling.

Patrick: I was thinking of starting a line in personalised coffins. Substitute pictures, as you might say. And more demand. And you would never meet them later in life and be struck dumb with embarrassment.

Gerald: M-m-marvellous. I w-w-want a b-b-black one, w-w-with f-f-flames, y-y-yellow and orange. W-w-with teeth. G-g-green s-s-snakes. T-t-teeth. T-t-teeth with t-t-teeth. And that b-b-big red t-t-tongue.

Patrick: I'll be delighted to do that for you, Gerald. I suppose I can do it on one of the handicraft courses, Mona?

Mona: But I don't think you're supposed to handle pointed instruments, Patrick.

Patrick: Paintbrushes aren't pointed. Someone else can make the coffin. And, from the look of him, someone had better make Gerald's pretty quickly.

So Gerald has tooth trouble as well, poor bastard. I remember them well, though I don't think they were ever disembodied. Teeth with teeth. Pretty far down the hole, I'd say. The flying foxes had very big teeth, sometimes with mice in them. Don't remember that they ever ate the mice. They just squealed all the time. That awful, high-pitched squeak. Like the bats. And they were everywhere. In every single room. You couldn't get away from them. I got quite fond of them in the end.

Well, they've gone now. And what do I have in their place? A great big enormous expanse of nothing. Nonsense all this talk about replacements. Could I replace Olivia with Bridget, for instance? Mona? No indeed, my God. Strange that she should be so absolutely, totally, incontestably unattractive. Probably why they chose her. No getting crushes on her. Julia doesn't like men, I imagine. Or knows nothing about them more likely. And as the girls are all substantially younger than my ghastly grandson don't want to be accused of cradle-snatching. And I'm not rich enough to be a sugar-daddy. Though there would be a satisfaction in making something out of Janice and Layne, a real something out of nothing job that would be. Never had totally impossible recruits. All volunteers and as keen could be. Lucky me.

But in fact we are in crisis. All of us. What do we do next? Our values are upside down. *Oolta poolta.* The agents, the publicity agents, the advertisers – they're the ones with the money. But it's all gift-wrapping. What do they do when there aren't gifts? Like packaging. Though I bet Barry could learn how to pack a shirt so that no one could unwrap it at all. Seventeen pins in my last one. And even then I missed one, as I found out when I sat down.

The world is ruled by economists and scientists and accountants. And people who can't tell fact from fiction.

What about that poll which found that the most famous engineer in Britain was someone on *Coronation Street*? They thought he was real. Just as I expect people think the Archers are real. Funny thing. When that series started there was no one in England even faintly like the Archers. A suburban family living in the middle of a field. Now everyone is like them. No country people left. The suburbanites take out injunctions to prevent cocks crowing at dawn. No romance. No excitement. No adventure. Humdrum porridge from the cradle to the grave. Nine to five week in and week out. No imagination. No initiative. Everyone eaten up with frustration and one can't blame them. Corroded. Rusty guts mean rusty brains.

And I'm frightened.

Yes. That's what I am.

Frightened.

Dudley: Because the Mice Men are in charge of everything.

Patrick: Who are the Mice Men, Dudley? They sound like part of Gerald's dream. Not yours.

Dudley: Did I say that?

Clarissa: You did. So tell us about them.

Dudley: Well, whenever you get a really nasty letter from some Council or other, saying you can't do whatever it is that you want to do, it's always signed by someone with MICE after his name.

Mona: Member of the Institute of –?
Julia: Cynical Egomaniacs.
Patrick: I wonder if it's only the British who instinctively oppose everything? All looking for reasons for not doing something. Always someone else's business to do everything.
Clarissa: We've been here already today. A nation of voyeurs, somebody said. But what about us in here? What can we actually do?
Mona: Well. Patrick thinks he can paint coffins. Barry can arrange flowers. Dudley can fight wars. Julia can –?
Julia: Preserve prints.
Gerald: S-sell f-f-flats. B-Banco de. Brazil. B-Barclays. B-Bilbao. O G-God yes. B-B-Bilbao. B-b-but wh-where's the h-h-hell is th-that?
Clarissa: Mona can teach, I suppose. I can't do anything and neither can the girls. Or Darren. But I bet Bridget has some hidden talent. Only she's not telling.
Bridget: Wrong. Quite wrong. I am. I am a very good. A very good cook. Why I'm so fat. Eating my own. Always delicious.
Patrick: I suppose you wouldn't think of offering the cook here a few hints?
Mona: Or taking a cookery class? I think you would find several pupils in this room.

Bridget: No. No. The effort. The struggle. And there must be. There must be a qualified. A qualified dragon there already.

Clarissa: So we're hardly equipped to run the ideal state.

Julia: No such thing, I think. A Marxist red herring. We are not ideal.

Dudley: And the whole is equal to the sum of its parts. What did God have in mind, I wonder?

Mona: Well, He gave us our intelligence, and our common sense, and expects us to use them.

Clarissa: He gave some of us an intelligence.

Julia: No, He gave us all an intelligence. But some are more willing to use it than others.

Patrick: And some of us have rather more of it than others.

Barry: Yer. Yer. Where's yer equality now?

Gerald: My f-f-foot's f-falling off again.

Barry: OK, old chap. Which one is it this time?

Gerald: S-s-same one. B-b-being chomped.

IX

CLARISSA

Barry: Bit better is it? Ow's the snakes? More tea if you want it.

Gerald: Y-y-yes, p-p-please. S-s-snakes are b-b-bad. D-d-don't like w-water.

Janice: Our angel says as I as an intelligence but never ad the chance to use it.

Julia: Well, you're a bit special, Janice. Though he's quite right, of course. There seems to have been a conspiracy against you. To prevent you using your mind, I mean. I think we can say that society, in its widest sense, has failed you completely. But that doesn't mean that you have to fail it.

Bridget: Never too late. Never too late to begin. Again. Try to forget. Forget to put the past behind you.

Mona: Do you think you could do that, Janice?

Janice: Could try. We ad a lotter leckshers from our angel afore we come ere an I foun myself thinkin that's all very well but what's in it for us?

Mona: O Janice, thank you, my cue at last. What I want to say, what I want to say to all of you, is that we have to stop thinking only about ourselves all the time. If we're honest, we can see that selfishness, self-obsession, self-indulgence, self-deception, self-pity, are our great problems. Once we admit that, we can go on.

Patrick: So – back to Step Two. What is it? A power greater than ourselves? I don't see how that's even faintly relevant in my case.

Mona: Perhaps not. In your case. But if you could see yourself, or your disputed talent, in relation to other people, you might not despise it so.

Patrick: I don't despise it. I despise me.

Julia: Forgive me, Patrick. But I have to say this. That is a kind of self-indulgence. In some ways the most selfish thing of all.

Patrick: So it's self-indulgent if I do paint and self-indulgent if I don't.

Clarissa: Who says it's self-indulgent if you do?

Patrick: Never you mind, Clarissa. It has been said, that's all.

Clarissa: But, Patrick, you have an enormous talent. I don't want to sound too like Mona, but if God gave you that talent then He expects you to use it.

Patrick: If I thought God had the arranging of this world then it might be worth the effort. As I don't, then why should I bother?

Julia: And what is your definition of selfishness?

Patrick: Very well. Touché, Julia.

Mona: Doing things for other people is a good beginning. Janice is already well on the way, because she's been looking after Layne all this time. And quite soon I expect Layne will start looking after her. Even Barry, after all, is looking after Gerald. And was helping Rosanna this morning.

Clarissa: And I took Uncle his cup of tea. It can't be as simple as that.

Mona: Great oaks from little acorns grow.

Clarissa: Very possibly. But it takes three hundred years.

Mona: All right. We know that you started your habit as the result of meeting that priest. But you had to be ready for it. You had to be willing to receive it, if you see what I mean. Why did you go to Switzerland in the first place?

Clarissa: Because I couldn't stand life at home, of course. All those girls. The constant stream. He wanted me out of the way.

Mona: And you didn't want to go?

Clarissa: O no. I wanted to go all right.

Mona: So it was a badly damaged ego that encountered the kinky old priest?

Clarissa: I suppose so. Yes. I think you could say that.
Dudley: Sounds more like a feeling of total insecurity to me.
Clarissa: Well, yes. Thank you, Uncle. You could say that too.

But what you can't say, or rather what I can't say, what I shall certainly never say to anyone at all, is what actually happened. All this brain-washing is a bore of the first water. Years and years since I thought about this, not because I don't want to but because I like to feel it is there, warm and cosy in some bottom drawer. Nothing to do with feeling guilty because the only thing I feel guilty about is not feeling guilty. Not feeling guilty at all. Why should one about a fantastic experience? A bit different from Layne and Janice. They really were forced into it. But I wasn't. Not with my sumptuous Daddy, my peerless Adam, my magnificent Daddam. What the press call a superb male animal, one of the handsomest, healthiest men in the world.

Of course I don't really think he knew it was me. Dusk. And in a hayloft. Could anyone want anything more romantic? He didn't speak. Didn't ask me who I was – why should he? That was where the evening's entertainment always happened. Just lay down on top of me and got on with it. And God it was marvellous. No question that practice makes perfect, in that department anyway. He took me right over the top that very first time and no one has ever done it since. And when he'd finished he just stood up, zipped himself up and walked off. I lay there in a sort of heavenly daze for about half an hour, I should think.

But of course he waited for me. He was there when I came out. My God, Clarissa, was that you? So I just said yes, and it was wonderful. I thought he was going to throw up. O God, what the hell have I done? And you were so good, so loving, as if you wanted nothing else. Well, I didn't, I said. I've been mad about you ever since I was about twelve. But little girls aren't supposed to fancy their fathers. I've never thought of you as my father particularly. You're very young, very gorgeous, very capable. No wonder everyone is queuing up to get into your bed. Or your hayloft. Just go upstairs and use the bidet. I'm on the pill, Adam. Didn't you know? And I really think he didn't.

Anyway he got very moral after that. Because, now that I come to think of it, I expect he fancied me too. Never thought of that before. How terribly funny. So it was off to hideous Lausanne very nearly the next day and we've hardly seen one another since. He pays for all this. Probably he feels guilty, that it's his fault which it only partly is. Takes two to commit incest after all. The unfortunate thing is that he was so good, so extremely well-endowed as the saying has it. But one can hardly ask for the measurements as soon as one meets a person. Bartholomew was hopeless and as for that disgusting little Darren. He showed me his yesterday. Just jumped out from behind a bush.

And what do you call that extremely small stalactite, I said. Calls im Tally-whacker he replies. What a huge name for such a tiny little object I said and went off as quickly as possible. And only then did the one bit of advice that my wonderful Adam has ever given me come into my head. Never criticise the equipment, he said. No man can stand it as he can do nothing about it. And I'm sure that if Darren had had a knife it would have been there, sunk in my bosom like Cleopatra. No, no, that was a snake. I expect one of Gerald's will get him in the end. Not that I should mind dying particularly. So long as it was quick.

All very well for Mona to go moaning on about selfishness and powers stronger than one. Does she really think I'm going to take a course in something when I get through this lot? If I get through this lot. Just not sure that I could do it myself. I think I could tell Patrick all this. Not unlike Adam, in type anyway. And about the same age. And if those paintings are anything to go by, he really does understand the female form.

Julia: But it is absurd to pretend that the past didn't happen. It modifies everybody's life in one way or another.

Patrick: And you carry your past with you wherever you go. Like Sinbad and the Old Man of the Sea.

Dudley: I didn't mean your own past. I mean the past, the historical past. We now have two generations who think the world began on the day they were born. Because they're not taught anything unless some trendy-lefty nut case thinks it relevant to their present way of life. So they can have nothing to compare their own lives with.

Patrick: Ignorance is bliss.

Clarissa: And comparisons are odious.

Julia: Yes, it is, and yes, they are. Clichés aren't always nonsense. Comparing one thing with another often just minimises them both.

Patrick: Because you can't discuss one thing in terms of another? We can't look at ourselves in terms of ourselves?

Mona: Well, thank you, Patrick. Back on course again.

Clarissa: An absolutely hopeless task, I should imagine.

Mona: Yes, if the subject decides not to co-operate. You threw a couple of golden apples at us and then went off into a brown study.

Clarissa: I was, of course, examining my past in terms of itself.

Mona: And what conclusion did you come to?

Clarissa: O, you don't have to reach a conclusion. Examination still in progress. Results are a long way off.

Janice: But if you carries your past with you always then you can't never get away from it. An it seems to me as you as ter get away from it if you're going to start again.

Julia: You can come to terms with it. If you can't forget it, you can try to forgive it. Or them.

Patrick: Quite difficult, for Janice.

Janice: Thing is, I got away. Bloody Raymond's dead. Ope bloody Brandy is too. Just ave ter stay outer London.

Mona: You got away from your cocktails.

Janice: Yeh. I did. Not as ard as you might think. Went through ell first few days. But then I were watching Layne an I says ter myself never again.

Layne: Yer. Yer. Never.

Mona: I call that a great triumph. You'll get a lot of help, here and elsewhere. But you have to be ready to accept it.

Clarissa: And you, Mona? Who helped you? What was your problem?

Mona: It was coke, Clarissa. Like Janice. But I had to lose a husband, and miscarry more than once, before I was prepared to ask for help.

Janice: Tell us about the usband, then. If you want to.

Mona: No, we haven't come here to talk about me. He was a marvellous man, clever and kind. But ambitious.

Patrick: So, not quite clever and kind enough. If he couldn't take you with him.

Really men are incredible. After listening to Janice and Layne one would think there was nothing left to learn. But to marry Mona. What did Dudley call it? The ultimate perversion. Morna frer Munchester. Except that she doesn't talk like that. Just a few oops from time to time when she forgets. Went on a course before she got here, I suppose. She was a schoolmistress before, of course. Still, the mind boggles. She looks weird enough with her clothes on.

We all look weird if it comes to that. Except Patrick. Patrick really doesn't look weird at all. I suppose for him it's just a question of being off the bottle and everything's all right. Except I don't think winos chop up their paintings like that. Don't think winos paint paintings in the first place. Sounds a bit more serious to me. Should think he would do anything on a down. Do himself in, cut his throat, cut somebody else's throat, burn the house down. Perhaps that's what he did. He needs a cheerleader of course. A female cheerleader. Why do I think Patrick doesn't really like other men very much? Sitting next to him it seems to come over in waves. A manic-depressive I called him and for once in my life I think I was right.

But Julia really is peculiar. A poet, how nice. My other neighbour. To look at I mean. That nose. And that long black dress. Still, at least it's clean which is more than you can say for Janice and Layne. Of course nothing shows the dust like black. Layne looks as if someone just found her – well, in a dustbin of course, but over a year ago. Hasn't changed her clothes since. Dear me, hope I'm wrong. Could be catching.

Gerald is about to go off his head completely I rather think. Sitting there twitching. He seems to have stopped going through the alphabet. Well, it would have taken the rest of the week to get to Z and we should all have had to sit here and listen. I don't think I care at all what happens to Gerald. Good-looking though. Well, quite. Only slightly cross-eyed and that may be a fault of the acid. Ruin your digestion one would think rather than making you squint. Good teeth. Seem to be his. Uncle I really love in a dutiful grand-daughterly way. Though how does one get dandruff on one's eyebrows? Get it to stay there I mean. And those terrible trousers. Flannel bags I think they called them and with very good reason. Salvation Army I would imagine, not Oxfam. Or perhaps he's just owned them for thirty years. Worn them, I mean.

And what do I look like? If I could feel ashamed I would feel ashamed, of the mess I have made of myself. But no shame. No shame left if there ever was any. That fucking Father Hubert. Not quite the right adjective for him. If anything ever happened there it happened under his cassock and with no help from me. What on earth is he doing now, do you suppose? Not on earth at all, probably. A little smoke in the sacristy all among the incense so no one would notice. While I told Madame that I was under instruction to enter her church. It was the primrose path all right. I think I really have done everything. Except snorting of course. Snorting is for beginners and I went straight into the third form.

Tall. Gawky now rather than elegant. I can do nothing with my hair. Thought it might be tactless to bring any real clothes down here. Black tights and picturesque rags seemed about right. But it's the emptiness. The nothing. The aching void, whoever said that. There is no excitement. Nothing to look forward to. Nothing to look back on. Do something for somebody else says Mona, more or less, not in those words exactly. Do what for whom? Don't see myself as a female cheerleader though those red women were really sensational. Always the same one, sometimes alone, sometimes with two or three of herself on the same canvas. They even turned me on faintly. The men must have been in agony. Luckily the catalogues were quite big. Chocolate box, said Bartholomew, whatever that meant. Chocolate boxes always have those terrible orange roses with corners. Or daffs or crysanths or glads. Certainly not naked red ladies. Perhaps I go to the wrong shop.

Gerald: M-m-my f-f-feet have gone. G-g-gone.
M-m-my l-l-legs are going. And I c-c-can't s-s-see.
B-b-better n-n-not to be able to s-s-see. B-b-blind.
B-B-B for b-b-blind. B-b-but I can't w-w-walk
w-w-without any legs.

Clarissa: Mona, can't you do something? Get a stretcher or something. Can't you see he means it?
Mona: Didn't think so at first. But perhaps you're right. Patrick. Barry. Would you very kindly go and get a stretcher? There should be one under the main stairs.
Barry: I'll go. Don't need two if it's empty. An I think it's a bit late ter stick the poor bugger's feet on again.
Mona: Perhaps a drink might help.
Gerald: N-n-no. B-b-bladder's b-b-bloody well b-bursting.
Patrick: I'll get the hot water jug. Not that one would notice any stains on this carpet.
Clarissa: Well really, Patrick. You think of everything.
Dudley: Good man in a crisis. You ladies can look the other way.
Janice: Don't be daft, Uncle. One of us'll ave to old the jug while you and Patrick get im into a nupright position. Never ad ter do this before, not even for a client. Bout the only thing I never done. Member that one, Layne? Oo ad ter stand on is ead. Defyin gravity e said if e stayed the right way up.
Patrick: I don't think the hot water jug is quite big enough.
Mona: Well, get something else. Anything. What a really terrible smell.

Clarissa: Perhaps that's falling off too. Putrefied.
Patrick: An almost empty teapot.
Julia: Not sure that sterilisation will be quite enough. Of the jug and teapot I mean. Have to throw them away.
Gerald: B-b-better now. Th-th-thank you. At least th-th-that's working p-p-properly.
Mona: Just sit still, Gerald. Barry will be back in a minute and I expect you're all right as long as you're sitting down. What were we talking about?
Julia: About the limits of happiness. Strangely irrelevant.
Clarissa: And what are they?
Julia: You can only be happy within the limits of your own life.You have to find them and accept them. Then, of course, you can expand them.
Bridget: Yes. Yes. You are absle. You are absolutely. You are right. Julia. A sense of portion. Prop. A sense of proportion is impotent. Portent. Very indeed.
Julia: Yes. Perhaps the most important thing. No, I shouldn't say that. Humour, perhaps. Everything is important only some things are more important than others.
Patrick: I think you mean equal, Julia. *Animal Farm*. And the entire country seems to have lost its sense of humour.

Julia: A very small misquotation. Equality is quite exploded. You only get it by reducing everyone to the lowest possible level. Ignorance and vulgarity become the norm. And what, as Lady Bracknell did not say, is the sense in that?

Janice: As appened though. To us.

Clarissa: So this is the classless society.

Layne: Yer. Yer. Right. Only way is up.

Clarissa: Terribly cheerful all of a sudden.

Janice: Well, why not? I enjoyed writin my story. Compiling my memoirs. Episode Two tomorrow, Mona. What you think?

Mona: I think Barry must have got lost. And Episode Two could hardly be more amazing than Episode One.

Janice: Course I can't rightly remember every single oner them clients. I'll juss do the ones as stand out. In my memory, I mean.

But what a marvellous idea. Why should brothels be only for men? Janice can obviously do anything so she could run it. Such a waste of glorious Daddam for instance, servicing all those stable ladies when he could make a fortune with no more effort. Adam At Stud. How many mares could he cover in a day, do you think? But perhaps it would be more difficult than that otherwise someone would have thought of it before. All those suburban ladies coming up for the sales. A very nice house a long way from

King's Cross. Covent Garden perhaps, not all that far. Where it all started, of course. Something very reassuring about WC2, if it is WC2. So safe having two loos. Respectable. The men of course would pay to be on the stud list. The ladies would pay to be covered and we should just sit back and shriek with laughter. Except that that's the one thing that one mustn't do. Janice must have ached with wanting to laugh. What do you suppose the one they called the Luton Turnoff really looked like? Don't think I could manage really. I'll just be the front lady in black satin. Black leather more likely. Which I actually think I would hate.

Here, at last, is the stretcher party. At least Gerald's legs still seem to be attached but he is a really most peculiar colour. What did Barry not call it? Eau de Nil. I daresay he would be one of our star performers.

Barry: I adter get it from the fizzios. Weren't under the stairs. An ercourse the dragon wouldn bleeve me wen I said we got this bloke oose legs ad fallen orf. But she copperated pronto wen I wispered the magic word ecstasy in er ear. She said take im straight to the doctor.

Mona: Yes, yes, of course. Just lay it down here and help Patrick to lower Gerald very gently on to it. He probably can't move himself at all. No, no, better the two of you take him under the arms and perhaps Janice and Layne would take his legs. That's right. That's very well done. Are you all right, Gerald? Comfortable?

Gerald: B-b-blind. B-b-blubbing. C-c-can't f-f-feel. C-c-can't f-f-feel a th-th-thing.

Mona: You'll be all right now. Patrick and Barry will take you to the doctor. And I think I'd better come to show you the way. I won't be long and please go on talking. I feel we have achieved something today.

X

DARREN

Clarissa: Such as what, do you suppose?
Janice: Such as gettin Layne to tell us what it were. Such as gettin Julia to say somethin. Uncle's told us bout is school. You told us bout your priest. Mona told us bout er marriage. We're talkin. All sept Darren. Aven't you got nothin tersay, then? Or is you too toffee-nosed ter mix in low society?
Darren: No I aint got nothin ter say. Don't know arfer them rubbish words. Aint got a mind no more neither. Took it away. Like Gerald's legs.
Clarissa: O, did you have one at some time? In some previous existence, perhaps?
Darren: Yer, it were another life. Nother world. Afore it all ganged up on me.
Dudley: Well, tell us, then, Darren. We can't listen if you don't speak.
Janice: It's still close, isnit, Darren? Not got buried yet.

Layne: Like you can feel it but can't tell it.
Darren: Yer. Like that.
Julia: So, what is it like? Is it like a long dark tunnel with a tiny point of light at the end?
Darren: Ner.
Dudley: No light perhaps?
Darren: Yer. No light.
Layne: An people crowdin roun yer all the time?
Darren: Yer. Crowdin.
Janice: But you're tryin ter run away from em?
Darren: Yer. Runnin.
Dudley: Can you tell us why you're running away?
Darren: Ner.
Julia: Because you can't tell us? Or because you don't know?
Darren: Cos I can't tell yer cos I don know.
Clarissa: Very clear.
Bridget: No, no, no. Clarissa. Be gentle. What was his? His habit. His problem. On what was?
Dudley: Quite right, Bridget, I think. Can you tell us what you were on?
Julia: He must think we're interrogating him.
Layne: We are.
Darren: Smackncoke.
Clarissa: My God, Darren, where did you get the money for that?
Darren: Pushin ercourse.

Janice: Dangerous that game. Did you gettin trouble with your gaffers?
Darren: Yer. Yer. Could say that.
Dudley: So he really is running away.
Darren: Yer. Yer. E really is.
Julia: And who is ahead at the moment, Darren?
Darren: Some is ahead an some is behind.
Clarissa: Very clear.
Janice: An you the squashed fly in the middle.
Darren: Not squashed yet. Got some squashin ter do.
Julia: Not here, I hope. Why did you come here?
Darren: Thought I'd be safe.
Dudley: Well, you are.
Darren: Depends what you mean.
Layne: Nobody'll get you ere.
Dudley: Only your own thoughts.
Clarissa: Darren hasn't got any of those.
Janice: Payin your own way are you?
Darren: Yer. Start again after.
Bridget: Yes, yes. Right. I do. Do hope you. Do. Do.
Darren: Thinks I were wrong that's all.
Layne: How wrong?
Darren: Cos you all come with me. Gangin up. You an Janice was runners for im weren't yer? I seed you afore often. Down the Bricklayer's. An Barrys is itman. Gerald's is boyfriend. Patrick's is brother. Mona n Uncle's perlice. Can tell by the way e walks.

Clarissa: And who am I, then?
Darren: Is bitton the side. Better make sure that Lorraine never gets a sighterv you. Long nails.
Julia: And I? What role are you giving me?
Darren: Reckon you're is mother.
Bridget: Now, now, Darren. No need to be. No rude to be need.
Julia: Gaunt and haggard I may be – how old is this person and what is his name?
Darren: Names Brucie.
Layne: We never ad no one called Brucie, Jan, did we?
Janice: Course not. E's barkin, that's all.
Dudley: Quite likely after that diet.
Clarissa: And Bridget? Who is she in this scenario?
Darren: One oo took ther money. Name's Muriel.
Julia: But where did all this happen?
Darren: I said. Down the Bricklayer's.
Clarissa: A well-known area of East London.
Darren: Nar. Nar. Bristol. Birmingham.
Janice: Right. Right. Remember that squat we ad, Layne, bang in the middle of Bristol n Birmingham? No wonder e remembers us so well.
Darren: Well I does so belt up.
Dudley: But surely you're a Londoner?
Darren: None o your bloody business where I comes from.
Julia: Quite right, it isn't. And as I think it may take some time to convince Darren that we're

on his side, perhaps we should stop questioning him so closely.

Dudley: Yes, yes, quite right. What were we talking about before?

Clarissa: How to achieve happiness through self-knowledge. Ironical as you might say. Irrelevant.

Dudley: No, I don't think I would say that.

Clarissa: Not ironical perhaps. But we certainly are irrelevant.

never be safe again   never   i were wrong   fraid i might be   but i ad ter getout getaway   an i ad this bitter money didn i   i never eard no one talker bout a detoxi whatever its called   sounded a doddle ter me   an if they never earder one they couldn be ere could they   but they is   they are   squashed fly janice says   smart girl janice   gettin that old bloke ter payer way ere   talk about cossly   couldn ardly bleeve my ears   food bloody awful   bed not too bad an not even safe   not my idea of a aven   or a notel

weird them all comin ere with new names   cant fool me though   that barry is dave an gerald is chris   an patrick is graham   don think i ever knowed what janice an layne was called   an as fer that effin clarissa her names rita   reckon i can best get back at bloody brucie through er   if im goin im takin er with me   that stupid graham   did e think i never saw im nickin that knife outer the kitchen   an did e forget it were bloody brucie taught me ter pick pockets proper was in my pocket almost afore it were in is an its a good knife strong sharp thin juss made fer gettin atween er ribs

cos i aint goin ter live with what theyve doneter me reckon i don mine bein topped if its quick knew ed fine out one day id been rippin im orf but i thought ed juss do it quick an down the builders four blokes unner canary worf but not bloody brucie ad me punchbagged an bloody buggered by is effin minders an im fourteen er them one arter another still bleedin not much butter bit let that be a lesson little shitbag an clear orf my manor so ere i am couldn fine the money could they unted igh an low they did didn know they was lookin fer a check book put it inner bank thought theyd never thinker lookin there an they didn brighteran that pissin chris membered which bank id put it in an got it out could stay ere for sevral months but i cant stand all this talkin an preachin and that fuckin moaner whoever named er got it right alright.

Julia: No, no, Janice, you have me all wrong. Everyone, everything, is open to misconstruction I suppose. But I do think health treatment should be free. And food and clothing and housing and transport and education. But until that can be arranged, which will probably be never, then we shall just have to continue to pay for them.

Dudley: The trouble is that when things belong to the people, they always have to be represented by a committee. Or a bureaucracy. Or a council. Or some other obstructive body. Tribunals. That kind of lark. The only true freedom is the freedom to starve.

Janice: If I ever runs across ole Two Peas again I must juss tell im what I thinks of is teachin. People is people all the way through. You juss aster learn oom ter avoid. What about that, Uncle?

Dudley: You have a great future, Janice.

getting right restless that rita   if she gets up im after er   callin my tallywacker a teeny tallactitie bloody insult   better frommer back with them bloody great tits in the way   at the back theres a thing called the aorter   don know what it is but if you gets it its curtains in a few seconds   juss under er leff shoulder blade   saw it marked up on a chart once   like them in the butchers oncer ponner time put it in an twist   special arranged fer cackanded bastards like i

Clarissa: Do we have to sit here until Mona gets back?

Dudley: She said she wouldn't be long.

Julia: What would you suggest?

Clarissa: I'm stifling. I want to go out. But at least I could open the window.

Julia: Open the French window. I don't know why Mona is so afraid we shall all run away.

Clarissa: Yes. You have very good ideas.

up she gets   up i gets   quick quick quick   drive it ome ard   no messin   christ what a lotter blood   an what a lotter bloody noise   screamin   yellin   shriekin   now me   up through the stomach   twist
bloody ell
didn reckon it would
urt

Janice: Darren, you bloody little creep you fuckin ponce what the ell dyou think you're bloody doin? O God, Layne, come an elp me with Clarissa. Take er ead.

Dudley: I don't think it's any good, Janice. You'd better go and get the doctor.

Julia: The top one we saw when we came in. With the wispy beard and green socks.

Janice: An what about bloody little Darren then?

Dudley: Just leave him where he is. He knew just what he was doing both times. Never thought anyone could be so quick. Or so efficient.

Layne: You mean they've gone?

Dudley: Yes. Yes, I'm afraid so. Even if there was a blood bank on the premises it wouldn't help. But, if it's any comfort to you, I don't think Clarissa can have known what happened. She'd be unconscious almost at once.

Julia: You've seen people die before, haven't you?

Dudley: Yes. Rather more often than I like to remember. But I'll say this for Darren. He was quick and effective. Almost a professional job.

Julia: So there was something he could do. We were wrong.

Dudley: Most of us are wrong. Most of the time. That's what makes it all so difficult.

Bridget: But I think he saved them. I think he saved them both. A lot. Take a deep breath. I think he saved them both a lot of anguish.

Gerald was dead before the doctor could get to him. Barry was convicted on one of three charges of inflicting grievous bodily harm and imprisoned for three years. Patrick, acquitted of arson, gave up all his artistic activities and is now a counsellor. Janice and Layne, after appropriate training and funded by Julia, opened a pets' beauty parlour, Chien Chic, at the bottom of Walton Street. Julia took over a small publishing company, the Islington Imprint, and made a tiny profit in her first year. Bridget recovered almost completely, became Weight Watcher of the Year and now runs her house as a refuge for battered wives. Dudley, now known as the Ancient Warrior, is still at Copsewood, a valuable listening post and an essential part of this establishment.

Mona
Copsewood